KNIGHT
of the RAILS

CHRISTINE WELLDON

Red Deer Press

PRAISE FOR KNIGHT OF THE RAILS

A thrilling read filled with a lot of heart.

~ *Jo Treggiari, YA author of* The Grey Sisters

I'm so thrilled that Canada finally has an answer to the great dust bowl balladeer, Woody Guthrie, and the fact that Billy is 13 years old, just learning to make his way in the world, makes his story that much more meaningful. A must read for the young and old.

~ *Chris Benjamin, author of* Boy With A Problem

Published in Canada by Red Deer Press,
209 Wicksteed Avenue, Unit 51, Toronto, ON   M4G 0B1

Published in the United States by Red Deer Press,
311 Washington Street, Brighton, MA 02135

Red Deer Press acknowledges with thanks the Canada Council for the Arts
and the Ontario Arts Council for their support of our publishing program.

Library and Archives Canada Cataloguing in Publication
Title: Kid Sterling / Christine Welldon.
Names: Welldon, Christine, author.
Identifiers: Canadiana 20200181785 | ISBN 9780889956162 (softcover)
Classification: LCC PS8645.E447 K53 2020 | DDC jC813/.6—dc23

Publisher Cataloging-in-Publication Data (U.S.)
Names: Welldon, Christine, author.
Title: Knight of the Rails / by Christine Welldon.
Description: Markham, Ontario : Red Deer Press, 2022. | Summary: "Thirteen-
year-old Billy Knight leaves home to 'ride the rails' across Canada during the
1930s. His encounters with a wide cast of characters -- including fellow drifters
and grifters; kid gangs; crooks; idealists; ragtag philosophers, and railroad
bulls; as well as everyday folk simply trying to get by--provide much more than
he bargained for. And for the first time, he realizes that riding the rails is not
just an adventure. It also speaks to the bravery of those drifting like tumbleweed
across the country and seeking a better life" -- Provided by publisher.
Identifiers: ISBN 978-0-88995-669-8 (paperback)
Subjects: LCSH: Drifters – Canada-- Juvenile fiction. | Homeless teenagers – Canada
-- Juvenile fiction. | Canada – History – Nineteen thirties -- Juvenile fiction. | BISAC:
YOUNG ADULT FICTION / Historical / General. | YOUNG ADULT FICTION / People
& Places / Canada.
Classification: LCC PZ7.W455Kni |DDC [F] – dc23

Edited for the press by Beverley Brenna
Cover and text design – Tanya Montini
Printed in Canada by Advanced Imaging & Integrated Media

www.reddeerpress.com

For Robert

*It was necessary to lie low and out of sight
until the train appeared and then run beside it
so as to leap and catch the handle bar...*

W.H. Davies ~ *The Autobiography of a Super-Tramp*

CONTENTS

CHAPTER 1

DUST

Billy stood ready, fingers crossed.

Down the track, a freight train waited in darkness. A figure trudged along the rails toward him, as a beam of light flashed—a railway guard searching for thieves who dared steal a ride—thieves like him!

"*Don't look here,*" he whispered from his hiding place. He hunched deeper into the shadows of the grain elevator. A startled rat scurried away. The guard kept his gaze on the train as he played the beam of his lantern over the shadows, bending to peer underneath each car, standing tall to shine his light up top. So close now.

Sweat trickled under Billy's collar and his heart thumped loud. The train sprang to life with a sudden rumble and a puff of white smoke.

Heading out! Westward bound!

Red lights flashed to green. Steam hissed like a kettle on the boil. Pistons pushed the rods that drove the wheels.

Boxcars thumped and banged as the train shuddered and edged forward. Billy stood ready to leave home, family, friends, everything he knew.

And all because of dust.

Where Billy lived, dust breathed and whispered like a live thing, looking for a place to settle. It coated tongues with grit, sneaked into milk cans, turned daylight into darkness, piled up at fence lines, and no rain ever fell. The wind worried at the dry topsoil like a mad dog and whipped it up into a black cloud, then hurled it from Saskatchewan to Alberta and back again.

On still nights whenever the wind let up from its constant moan, Billy had lain awake and listened for the train whistle from the nearby track. The rhythm of the steel wheels beat into his head and something inside him thrilled to its call. "Come see the world!"

A few months back, that rhythmic song had beckoned his older brother, and Ed had slipped out in the middle of the night and left a goodbye note on Billy's pillow.

I'm riding the rails, heading west. I'll write soon as I got a job and get settled.

Ed had left before the worst happened—the loss of their family farm to dust and drought. Tomorrow, his parents were moving into town. Tonight, while they slept, Billy had dressed, packed a sack with some spare clothes, a blanket, a loaf of bread and an apple, and left a note on the kitchen table.

Don't worry. I'm heading west. I'll be back when I got a hundred dollars and a car.

Now Billy crouched to spring out, feeling his toes squished tight inside his brother's cast-off shoes. The train picked up speed. The guard had turned and was headed back to the station.

All clear!

Go!

He sprinted forward, lit by the yellow glow of the station light, and ran to catch up with the train as he searched for some place to grab on and climb up. Along the line he spied a boxcar with its door partly open. The railway guard turned at the flurry of motion. Saw him. Broke into a run.

"Hey! You there!"

Caught!

No time to wait. No time to wait. No time to wait, pulsed the beat of wheels on rails. Fast, faster. Here it comes! Now or never. Grab on. Grab on. GRAB ON!

Right hand gripped the edge. Feet moved to catch up. Sack tossed inside. But the train began to race against him. Too fast! Feet too close to the wheels! *Don't pull me under! Help! Help me!*

Gasping. Warm piss down his leg.

Running steps behind him. "Hey! Get away, you bastard!"

The guard's club glanced off his shoulder, stung.

Billy tensed for the brutal grip of hands pulling him down to shove him under the wheels till he was chopped like sausage meat. He heard whimpering. His own.

I'm gonna die! Dammit! All over before I even started!

A hand reached out of the car, clamped onto his arm, hauled him up and flung him inside.

"What the hell you up to, durn fool!"

Billy lay sprawled on the rattling floorboards. Faint moonlight showed a figure framed in the doorway, stocky body, thick legs braced for balance, bushy beard, and a voice rising harsh above the rumble and bang of the car.

"Don't you know nothin', kid? Never catch out on the fly, 'less you wanna die young."

The man turned away with a snort. "Greenhorn, fellas!"

Billy sat up and wiped his face with his hand, felt a wetness there. Blood. Just a scratch and nothing broken. Delight welled up inside him. *Still alive!* He stood up and found his balance on the rocking train, then stumbled to the open doorway. "Ha ha! Can't catch me now!" he shouted down the track, laughing and waving as the light from the guard's lantern faded into the night.

He turned to the man inside and a whiff of tobacco, piss, and smoke hung between them.

"That guard almost got me! Thanks, mister!" He rubbed his throbbing shoulder where the club had landed.

"Lucky for you I got you first. How old are you, ten?"

He squared his shoulders. "Thirteen."

"So what do you call yourself?"

Billy planted his feet firmly to counter the bounce of loose planks.

"Lucky, I guess."

Laughter from one side of the car. Billy stared that way into the gloom. Two shapes sat hunched in the corner.

"Name's Billy Knight."

"Lucky's a good handle. Never give anyone your real name," the man scoffed. "So, Lucky, that's Bud," he continued, pointing at one of the shapes. "That's Sam. I'm Mac. So you callin' yourself a 'bo?"

"Sure, I'm a 'bo." He shrugged and shoved back a lock of hair. A passenger train roared along the opposite track, heading east. Its lit carriages brightened the gloom in their boxcar and Billy caught a glimpse of sleeping passengers, comfortable in plush seats.

"You got red hair," noted Mac as the train passed on by with a fading clatter. "Same colour as mine till it turned white, thanks to Prime Minister Bennett." He hacked and spat. "What're you doin', hoppin' a freight, kid like you?"

15

"Lookin' for work, headin' west."

"This your first catch out, huh?"

Billy nodded. He would just have to put up with the man's mockery. Mac had rescued him from certain death, so let him have his fun till he got tired of it and let him be. But Mac hadn't yet finished with him.

"So now, what you carryin', there?" Mac moved close to stare long and hard at his sack of belongings, pretending confusion, then bent to pick it up.

"Hey! That's mine!" Billy made a grab for it, but Mac jerked it out of reach.

"Ha! I see what this is." He nodded his head slowly to show understanding had dawned. "You tryin'a make a bindle! It could do with some fixin'. You got some rope? Here. Let's tie this sucker up and do it right."

In the flashing lights of a railway crossing, Billy protested as the man pawed through his scant belongings, fingered the bruised winter apple, "Don't touch that!"—sniffed the loaf of bread, "Leave that alone!"—shook out the shirt as Billy made a grab for it but Mac blocked him with his elbow, examined his wool socks neatly darned by his mother, then shoved it all back into the sack and rolled it up inside Billy's blanket. He pulled a length of rope from his own bindle, tied the bedroll with a twist or two, fastened a loop, slung it over the boy's good shoulder and stepped back, satisfied.

"*Now*, you got a bindle! Next stop, Saskatoon. We'll unload and catch out again. Stick with us and learn somethin'." Mac shrugged and turned away. "Or not. Up to you."

Job complete, Mac sat down beside the others, lit a corncob pipe and passed it along, ignoring Billy. The men jawed and jabbered and bickered, and lazed like they were in a boat on a lake instead of a racketing boxcar. Billy stood awhile and aimed his rear toward the doorway to dry the seat of his pants. Then he sat like the others till the bounce of loose planks rattled his bones and he stood again.

As the sun showed its first light, he could see the men clear. Bud looked regular enough, pants not too shabby, eyes curious, mouth ready to laugh. Sam owned a hacking cough and a blank stare. His eyes fixed on Billy for some time till they shifted and fixed on a gap in the planks. Mac's bushy brows moved like furry caterpillars, his mouth hidden beneath layers of beard and whiskers as he talked enough for all of them, making up corny jokes that ended with a loud "Haw!"

The rising sun lit the dry prairies and empty farmhouses. Billy looked out through the open doorway and saw the same dust that had choked his own family's wheatfields, changing their colour from a rich gold to a lifeless brown and grey. The same tumbleweed piled up against walls and fences. He saw a farmer and his wife bent over a ruined wheat crop. The two looked up at the passing train and waved to Billy, and as he waved back, he felt their sadness.

His thoughts turned to his mom, and how she could not stand the sight of the grey film covering her curtains, chairs, tables, and bedclothes.

"Don't bring that dust in here," she would scold as she stood at the sink, scrubbing everything clean. "Get out and brush it off before you come inside!"

By the slant of the sun, he figured his mom and dad were up and about now, preparing to leave the farm and move into town. Maybe they'd found his note on the kitchen table. His mom was a worrier and wouldn't take it well, but his dad would understand.

"Get away from there, Lucky!" Mac shouted.

Billy startled, jumped away from the doorway, lost his balance and fell backward. He scrambled up from the floor, expecting more mockery but heard only a snicker or two.

"Another lesson for ya. Don't stand at the door. Train brakes, you're gone, and I mean gone!"

As if to prove his point, the train slowed with a squeal of brakes and the door where Billy had been standing crashed shut with a deafening squeal. Mac had bossy ways, but Billy figured he could put up with him if it saved his life now and again.

Mac hauled on the door to slide it open, glanced out at the passing scene.

"Station stop, Saskatchewan River, Saskatoon," he announced. "Time to unload! We're gonna have to use our pegs and walk across."

Billy saw a steel trestle bridge up ahead, the letters CN painted on a fence along the pedestrian walkway, and a wide glittering river that flowed beneath.

"Whyn't we just stay on the train?" It would be grand to ride in style across that river. He stared out at the skyline of the great city. His own hometown, Venn, was just a hiccup compared to this!

"Don't you know nothin'?" Mac's brows drew together to show astonishment at Billy's stupidity. "Always unload before the train stops at a station, dummy! Them bulls'll be waitin' up ahead in Saskatoon. They find you stealin' a ride, they'll throw you in the calaboose if they don't shoot you first." Mac jabbed his thumb at his chest. "Watch me. I'll show yuh how it's done."

The train slowed to a running pace. Mac stood at the doorway, knees bent in a half-crouch as he faced forward, but he turned to bark some instructions at Billy.

"Check the ground is clear up ahead. Throw out your bindle first. Jump and keep your feet movin' like you're runnin' on air before you land. Got it?"

Bud and Sam got up with groans and mutterings and stood ready.

"Do it wrong, and you got your ticket to heaven," Mac warned.

Billy gripped his bindle, knuckles white, and got in line. At home, he loved to leap out of the hayloft into the stack below, howling like a coyote. This couldn't be any harder. He watched as Mac tossed out his bindle, and giving a flash of the young man he used to be, graceful and limber, he leaped. Bud and Sam showed less agility but, feet running in air, they kept upright when they landed. Came Billy's turn, his nerves jumped like a colt. A second blast of the train whistle and he gulped air, looked out for a smooth patch of ground below, tossed out his bindle, howled for the thrill of it ... and took the leap.

—· CHAPTER 2 ·—
HOW IT'S DONE

And landed clean! He stumbled but ran faster to counter the forward momentum. Easy, now he knew how. His steps slowed to a walk, and the exhilaration drained out of him as a heavy tiredness began seeping in. He'd lost a night's sleep.

The end boxcar and caboose passed him by as the freight train rumbled on across the bridge, its noise and rattle fading to a hush. The three hobos trudged ahead along a pedestrian path over the river. Mac's voice drifted faintly back to him, and the man's arms made sawing motions to stress some point or other, an occasional "Haw!" sluicing the quiet.

"Hey, wait for me!" Billy shouted, expecting them to turn and beckon him to join them. Nothing came. No matter. He'd started this adventure alone—he'd carry on that way. He reached the far side of the bridge, trailing behind as the three stepped along the paved road ahead. They turned onto a strip of tarmac that skirted the city all spread out beside the river. The windows of its tall buildings flashed in the sun and the faint sound of city traffic hummed.

The warm sun on his cheek cheered him and with the morning so fresh and new, all his senses were tuned in to this new journey. Excitement bubbled up inside and he let it out with a jump and a skip, then chuckled at the strangeness and wonder of it all.

He kept the men in sight. Underfoot, the hard tarmac became a dirt road that wove among brown shrubs thirsting for rain. Billy felt a thirst of his own and fished in his bindle for his apple. As he bit into it, the explosion of flavour and juicy sweetness spurred him on.

The men reached a siding where rails led off this way and that in several directions. Billy was only a short distance behind now. He followed across a set of tracks to gaze at a landscape of rundown shacks and lean-tos. Close by, a shopfront displayed a red and white barber pole, offering a shave and a haircut. Alongside the rails, neat stacks of iron pilings stood in a crumbling landscape of randomly flung railroad ties, and broken bottles. A worn canvas shoe perched half-burned in a pile of ashes. It seemed the railway had smashed its way through and left only debris in its wake.

Mac and the others stared through the window of an eatery.

"Best Little Diner in Town," read the painted sign. "Breakfast 30 cents."

The scruffy cinder block building, its blue paint trim peeling away, seemed to have given up all pretense of being the best at anything. But the thought of a filling meal already put a warmth into Billy's stomach and he moved closer. Mac turned to him at last.

"Go on into that beanery, then, Lucky," he called. "Get us some grub."

"Don't got the money." Billy clenched his toes to feel the edges of the dollar hidden inside his shoe—his own private stash.

Mac seemed to be entering a loose partnership with him, as temporary as the bits of old newsprint drifting around them in the breeze. Good enough for now but no permanence to it. Inside the diner, Billy could see a couple of men at the lunch counter, sipping from china mugs and chatting together.

Bud and Sam wandered away muttering about a shave and a wash. Mac guffawed.

"Watch out for Cupid's itch," he called after them, then turned back to eye the customers.

"We don't need money to eat," said Mac. "I'll tell you how it's done."

"Nah. Don't want to beg," said Billy.

"Don't have to. See those two fellas sittin' there drinkin' coffee? Put on a *sad* face. Go sit between 'em and ask the waitress if she got any work for you and your poor old dad, so you can earn some coins and pay for breakfast. You'll get us free grub. Gua-ran-*teed*."

Billy hesitated. His dad would frown at begging. So would his brother Ed. But his stomach gave a loud rumble and Mac gave him a gentle shove.

"Tell 'em your pa's out here waitin' and too shy to come inside," he urged in a wheedling tone. "You wanna eat, don't you? Put your pride in your pocket and off you go."

Billy took a breath and pushed open the door. The smells of breakfast cooking drew him in. The young waitress looked up and smiled a welcome that pulled him to the counter.

He gulped and began. "I'm real hungry, Miss. My dad's too ashamed to come in. He don't like to beg."

He looked into her eyes and saw kindness there. He pointed toward Mac outside, hat in hand, nose against the glass, teeth bared in a smile that didn't seem much at home on his face. Across the street, Billy glimpsed Bud and Sam loafing outside a rooming house talking to a woman.

"So, maybe you got a job for us so's we can earn some pennies and get some breakfast?"

The men at the counter looked him over. They didn't look too well off themselves, stubble on their faces and dressed in stained work clothes, lunch buckets at their feet.

"Ah, give him the breakfast special, Jane, and another for his dad," said one. "It's on me."

The woman nodded and went through swinging doors to the

kitchen. Billy stood awkwardly, twisting the rope on his bindle. In spite of feeling some shame at having to lie and beg, it felt good to soak up the warmth of the diner. Jane soon returned with two plates piled with ham and eggs and toast, placed them on the counter and poured him a tall glass of milk.

"Sit down, hon. And tell your dad to come on in and eat," she said.

But Mac was already inside the door, his eyes lit up at sight of the loaded plates.

"Thank you, fellas. Thank you, lady. My boy here could sure use a good breakfast. We ain't havin' much luck on the road."

The men wished them better luck, paid, and made their way out. Billy sat down and forked into the meal. Mac lowered himself onto the stool beside him, closed his eyes, bowed his head, and gave Billy a sharp poke with his elbow.

"Say your grace, son."

Billy figured it was all for show, but he put down his fork to play along and muttered the little prayer his family always recited at supper. Mac looked real proud he'd raised his son so well. As they dug in, he chatted with Jane who joked along and fussed over Billy.

"What a fine young man you are!" She leaned over the counter to touch his hair. "You got such lovely red hair. You got a temper to go with it?"

Billy looked into her eyes, smiled and felt his face flush with heat. He shoved food into his mouth to hide his shyness, then wiped the plate clean with his slice of bread.

"Time to make tracks." Mac lifted his cap and bowed. "Mighty grateful for the meal, Miss!"

Billy turned to thank her again. "You got beautiful eyes," he blurted, surprising himself. Her eyes were a rich brown like the eyes of his pet horse, Sadie. "I'll never forget you."

Jane chuckled. "Wait a minute." She cut two slices of angel cake and wrapped them up. "Something for the road."

Outside, Mac chortled and wheezed and stuffed cake into his mouth. "You got bee-u-tiful eyes!" he mocked. "You're learnin' real fast, Lucky."

It wasn't a line, I meant it, thought Billy. He felt a sharp tug in his gut, thinking about Sadie. He remembered the feel of her soft nose and warm breath in the palm of his hand whenever he brought her a carrot. His father couldn't afford to keep her and had sold her months ago. She'd been getting so skinny with little to eat except for Russian thistle or straw flavoured with molasses, and oats when they weren't scarce.

He buried these thoughts as he walked along with Mac for some distance past the railroad siding till they stood beside the track. As if on cue, a locomotive puffed toward them, moving slow.

"Let's go," said Mac, his steps quickening.

Billy glanced about him. "Any bulls around?"

"This ain't the main line, Lucky. Pretty quiet right here. You and me'll be partin' ways when we get to Leney. I got family there. Okay. Get down ..."

They crouched together in the tall grasses as the train moved closer. A rustling to Billy's left caught his attention, another sound behind, and again off to the right. In a flash, men of all shapes and sizes scurried by.

Billy's mouth hung open as he stopped to stare, but Mac yanked on his arm.

"Move!"

With no time to spare, the two of them ran for an open car. But others outpaced them, raced ahead, pushed by to scramble up inside, or climb onto the roof—men in shirttails, and overalls, shabby suits; rags and tatters that had seen too many greasy spoons and roadside beds—all in a hurry.

Glimpses of a red waistcoat and watch chain flashed past, then a face with one eye missing, flesh puckered, then came a beard, long and tangled in a gaunt face. This one had dirty chewed fingernails. That one wore boots flapping, toes peeking out. There, rosy cheeks smudged with grime. Here, pale eyes in a skeletal face, clean but deathly white.

Up they all climbed or leaped or shoved. Mac clambered in and hauled Billy in alongside. More and more men appeared, chasing the train as it gained speed, hands gripping, some losing the race, looking up at Mac and Billy perched safely inside a boxcar, "Give us a hand!" Mac dragging them up and in, one by one, till the car was full, with room for no more and the train moving at full tilt, westward bound.

"Where you been ..."

"... can't find ..."

"... useless sons a ..."

"... nothin' at all ..."

"... some work ..."

"I tell ya ..."

"God, help ..."

"... all I ask ..."

Their voices rose and fell around him—plaintive, questioning, disbelieving, and finally, lulling as he curled into a corner and fell into a restive sleep. He awoke now and then to hear Mac's throaty rasp calling out the towns that passed by in the late afternoon— "Farley!" "Grandora! How did Grandora get its name?" he asked of anyone who might care to listen. "Newlyweds, Dora and Don, got off the train here, started their married life. 'Ain't this place grand, Dora?' says Don. Grandora! HAW!"

Along the alphabet railway they chugged, through Hawoods, Ivana, Juniata, Kinley, little villages strung out across the prairies like bells on a harness.

When Billy woke up, he looked around for Mac, perhaps lazing at the other end and smoking a pipe. The boxcar held twenty or so men. But Mac no longer sat among them, nor was he standing at the doorway—a hobo shepherd—helping other drifters inside. A man noticed Billy searching and gave him the answer with a jerk of his thumb.

"He unloaded back there a-ways."

Billy figured this was the hobo way. For a while, he and Mac had fallen into a steady rhythm, their tracks running side by side. Now they wound away in different directions. He found himself alone again.

—· CHAPTER 3 ·—
A LETTER HOME

Billy felt as thirsty as a well gone dry. He'd had nothing to drink since his diner breakfast, and he couldn't take another minute of a thirst that emptied his mind of everything but this clawing need for water. The train dropped speed to an almost walking pace as it rumbled uphill to round a bend. At the sight of some houses scattered alongside the track, Billy moved to the open door. Someone in one of those houses might give him water if he asked politely.

He checked the ground ahead for a clear path, then knees bent, he threw out his bindle and leaped, feet running in air to land clean on the gravel bank alongside. The train passed him by and he returned the lazy wave of a hobo sitting up on top. He left the track and headed for a gravel road, listening for a sound of trickling water from a nearby stream or creek, but the silent, wide-open prairie stretched around him. Only the harsh sounds of crows broke the silence. The railway track wound into the distance, its steel rails glinting beneath the afternoon sun.

Up ahead stood a white clapboard house. A woman stared at him from the verandah. She was peeling potatoes and dropping long ribbons of peel into a tub at her feet. She had a hard look to her, a frown on her forehead, mouth tight. He hesitated a second, bindle on his back, fists in his pockets, and she stood to get a better look at him.

"You looking for something?" she called out, eyes narrowed with suspicion. Her brown hair was pulled up so tightly in a bun that it gave her face a pinched look.

"I'm real thirsty," he called. "Just come to ask for some water, if you got some."

"Wait there."

She lifted the pot of potatoes and went into the house with it, the screen door slammed shut and he waited at the bottom of the steps and looked around. An axe sat wedged in a stump over at the side of the house, and beside it a small pile of wood was stacked, ready for chopping. She came back out with a pitcher of water and poured him a cup. He moved to the steps, his hand outstretched for the cup, gulped it down and she poured him another.

"Where you from?"

"Venn," he said, lifting the cup to drink, his thirst not yet quenched.

She nodded. "Long ways from here. You a runaway?"

"No, ma'am. Just looking for work."

"Maybe you want to earn a few pennies?" she asked. "Finish splitting that wood by the house and I'll give you a quarter and something to eat."

"Sure, I can do that ma'am."

She led the way around the side and on past the small heap of wood. At the back of the yard, he saw a whole big pile of wood for chopping. It would take him hours to get through all that and he looked back at her, dismayed. "This pile?"

She nodded and didn't seem to notice his surprise at the size of it. "Fill up that barrel with kindling and then come onto the porch for lunch."

There was a big empty barrel nearby, so he picked up the axe and began to chop the wood into kindling. He put his back into it and his arms ached at this sudden hard work after a poor night's sleep. That axe blade was dull but he kept at it. She watched a while, then nodded, satisfied. All this work for just a sandwich and a quarter! Hardly worth the trouble, but now he felt hungry so he kept on.

As the minutes passed and the sun beat down on him, each piece of kindling tossed into the barrel seemed to sink into a bottomless hole. His back was strong and his palms tough from his farm labour, but even so, it would take forever to fill that barrel.

"Hell, I'm gonna run off, forget the lunch and the quarter," he muttered. But he soon had a better idea and looked over at the side window to make sure she wasn't watching. He placed a few long pieces over the top of the barrel, now only half full, and stacked some small pieces on top to make it seem filled up to the brim. He hoped he had fooled her. At that moment, she came around the side of the house to check his progress.

She eyed his work. "Okay," she said. "That's enough, you can sit up on the porch and I'll bring your lunch."

He sat down at the porch table, relieved to sit in the shade, and noticed a stack of writing paper and envelopes lying on it. She came out with a tray of food and cleared the papers to one side. She placed the tray down and Billy moved his chair in and looked at the spread. There were fried potatoes and a piece of ham, coleslaw, and a big wedge of apple pie with some cold apple cider to wash it down.

She lowered herself into a chair with a sigh of relief. "What's your name, boy?" she asked as he began to gobble up the food.

"Billy."

"You oughta be in school," she said.

"School shut down early spring. No money to pay the teacher."

"You a farm kid?"

He nodded. As he ate, he told her about himself, and she listened with a quiet interest that encouraged him to share more. He explained how the whole world had started turning upside down a few years ago when he was around eight years old. He'd been borrowing a book from the library shelf in the village store, and he overheard customers talking about a stock market crash.

"Ran home, told my dad a real bad accident happened, some cows got killed in a barn crash or something. I guessed they were prize cows, I told him, 'People are jumping out of *windows*, they're that upset.'" Billy shook his head, remembering the start of their problems. "Found out it wasn't cows. It was people banked their money and lost it all. Then the hoppers, and no rain … our crop kept going bad."

"It's like that everywhere, son," she offered. "We lost some of our savings, too. You want to be a farmer like your dad?"

"Yes, ma'am. I want a farm of my own." He told her about working the land. "We got a tractor, a John Deere. Me and my brother Ed like firing her up, tinkering with the engine when it breaks down."

He stopped his flow of words. They'd lost the farm, tractor and all. Ed had left, and it was hard to say how much all that hurt, or explain that farming was more than just some soil out there to plant seeds in. The images in his mind painted a better picture than his words ever could—how steam rose in the cool evenings from a freshly plowed field, the first young green stalks of wheat pushing up, the golden sweep of it and the bounty of summer harvest, the earth resting under winter snows and pulsing with the urge to grow. It was all as much a part of him as the hard calluses on his palms.

"Well, I used to like fixin' that tractor engine," he said again, and shrugged to pretend it didn't matter. "Looks like that's over. The bank took everything."

She pursed her lips and slowly shook her head. "I've been writing to the prime minister asking for help for the people around here, but he's a mean old bastard." She picked up an envelope from the pile to show him. It was addressed to R.B. Bennett. "Never got an answer, yet, but I'll keep writing him."

He ate the last mouthful of pie and hoped for more.

But instead, the woman pushed a square of writing paper and a pencil toward him. "Your mother must be worried sick about you. Write her a note to say you're well fed and not to worry." She had a way about her, the kind that if she told you to do something, you must snap to and do it. So he took the pencil and paper, thought for a moment, and wrote, *Don't worry. I'm fine and eating good. Your son Billy.*

She read the note, nodded, folded it and told him to write his address on the envelope and she'd put it in the mail with the rest when she went into town today.

"Thanks, ma'am," he said and picked up his bindle.

"Here's your money." She reached into her apron pocket and held out a dollar bill.

He could hardly look her in the eye. He stared at the bill. "I can't take that dollar. I didn't finish all the job."

"I know that," she answered, a sparkle in her eyes. "I got children of my own liked to shirk their chores. I was watching you make that barrel look full. Take it anyway and good luck."

He took the dollar and she turned and went inside without another word.

He called a thank you, then set off with a full stomach, an extra dollar in his pocket, and lots of puzzlement and wonder about how some people *look* hard, but aren't always so on the inside. It was like his dad always said—good surprises can happen, even in tough times.

He remembered one night a few months ago when his dog had died. His dad had helped him bury his pet near the slough where Digger always loved to crouch sniffing for ducks, or listen to rustlings in the wild grasses. Afterward, Billy had gone walking with his father over prairie fields.

There was not much talk between them, and Billy, sunk in gloom, had caught himself searching for a glimpse of his dog, could almost hear him scampering about. He'd stood a while with his dad to look up at the sky and seen the flash of a shooting star.

"There goes Digger," said his dad.

Billy scoffed, but his father gestured widely at the sky.

"Well how do you know? Lots of wonder all around us even when the going is tough. Always be open to surprises, son."

That talk had stayed with him. Looking up and seeing that sudden flash of light had helped put the cap on it for Billy. For sure, Digger was travelling on to a different place and saying a last goodbye. And at this minute, with that extra dollar in his pocket and the kindness of a stranger, he appreciated his dad's advice even more.

When Billy had walked some distance down the road, his eyelids grew heavy from tiredness and his legs moved slower with every step. He crossed the ditch into a field, and lay down in some brush for a nap, his jacket beneath his head. The crickets were droning around him and it didn't take long for him to sink into a deep slumber. He woke up cold and shivering to find the sun had lowered in the sky. Where did the day go?

He began to walk west along the dirt road. The hills, fields, and distant forests stretched to the horizon, silent as a graveyard and not a hobo in sight. A sharp gnawing began in his stomach, like hunger, but this was something very different—the frightening feeling of being out here all alone, without a friend to talk to, and nowhere warm to go.

He felt sunk so low he began to think he might hop on a freight going back east, get back to his folks but he'd look real stupid to give up after one day on the road and no hundred dollars or a car to show for it. He *had* to keep going. "Pull yourself together," he muttered. "Gotta hop another freight or find a place for the night. A barn or a boxcar, maybe."

He plodded along the track, looking behind him for a train. He hoped to hear its low rumble, and now and again, he laid his hand on the rail to feel for a vibration that never came. A hush had spread over the land, the birds were quiet and no breezes blew. The sun hovered at the horizon. He imagined something in the fields watched him. He felt eyes on his back. Behind him, a twig snapped, loud as a gunshot in that stillness. He swung around to look. Nothing there. He walked on, moving faster, and his thoughts turned once again to home.

About now, his mom and dad would be sitting down to a hot supper at his aunt and uncle's rooming house in town, then enjoying a play on the radio, some new jazz music, or maybe a baseball game. He and Ed always listened to the boxing together and wished they could see right inside the radio to watch the heavyweights. Maybe he would meet his brother on the rails some day.

He heard a sound, a shuffle, or was it just the wind sighing in the dry grasses? The prairie was a lonesome place and who knew what lived out in those forests and fields. Wolves, maybe. Killers, even. He jumped at the sound of footsteps. Somewhere behind him. An uneven pace—whatever was out there, he wouldn't wait around to find out. He broke into a run and his steps echoed on the road. Was someone or something keeping pace with him? He stopped. Swung round. Listened again.

"Hey, kid!"

A few hundred yards behind him, a hobo limped with quickening steps. Up ahead, the strains of a mouth organ played a merry, bouncy tune. He scampered around a bend and glimpsed wisps of smoke curling upward. He came on a clearing at the side of the road, strewn with heaped blankets and scattered belongings. A few men bent over a firepit to add sticks as flames leaped. The aroma of something delicious drifted toward him. Further in, a fellow sat on a stump and played a mouth organ, his toe tapping in time to the music.

Billy hesitated at the side of the road, then walked on in.

— · **CHAPTER 4** · —

JUNGLE

At the edge of the camp, an old man with long grey hair peered into a shard of mirror hung on a tree and shaved the stubble on his chin. He hummed along to the cheerful music, grabbed his cheek and stretched it out to catch every last whisker with his blade. The lines of his face seemed as deep as the cracks in the parched prairie.

He turned in Billy's direction, cloudy eyes seeking him out. He reminded Billy of his old dog Digger, half-blind and hard of hearing.

"Lookin' for somethin'?" the hobo asked by way of introduction.

Billy moved in closer and the man's eyes focused on him. His feet were tied with rags to stand in for shoes, his pants and shirt threadbare and hanging loose on his bony frame. He seemed set on getting that shave to make up for the rest of him being so shabby.

"Something sure smells good," said Billy.

"Hungry? We're sittin' down for a knee-shaker, kid. What's your name?"

"Bil ... Mac." Billy remembered the hobo rule to keep his real name a secret. Mac seemed as good a name as any.

"You got some food for the pot?" The fellow turned his attention back to his mirror, leaning close to finish off and wipe away the soap with his sleeve.

Billy looked behind him along the road. No one there. He drew in toward the campfire.

"I got a loaf of bread."

The man jerked his stub of a razor at the fire. A big pot hung from a small teepee over the flames. "Take a seat."

He walked into the camp feeling all grown up at being invited into that crowd. He tried to forget that just minutes before he'd been running like a scared rabbit, and had pissed his pants a while back. He moved close to the fire. Two hobos were just sitting down for warmth, tin plates and cans at the ready. They glanced his way and nodded a greeting.

Billy sat down across from them, and the fire's warmth offered him some comfort and safety. At that moment, his pursuer appeared on the road. The man was of medium height, not old, not young, brown hair streaked with grey and stubble on his chin, but tidy, hair cut neatly, good leather shoes. His eyes swept around the camp and fastened on Billy.

"Can I step in, Boss?"

"You got summat for the pot?"

"Sure, I got these," he said, pulling out two ears of corn from his bindle.

"Come in, then. What do they call you?"

"Fingy."

He limped toward the fire, showing no interest in Billy. "Gimme some room, fellas. Let a tired old 'bo in."

The men shifted and Fingy sat across the fire from Billy.

More men ambled in and offered a turnip, some potatoes, a carrot for the pot. Boss seemed to be mayor of this place. It reminded Billy of a colony of prairie dogs he'd once spied upon— the top dog sitting outside his burrow to bark his orders and alarms and gossip to the others, just like Boss.

One hobo walked up with nothing for the pot.

"Well, go into town," said Boss. "Find a cabbage or steal somethin' if you want to eat tonight."

"Okay, Boss," said the fellow and walked off, muttering, "Old buzzard ..."

Billy sat drooling with hunger. His fellows around the fire gave him pitying looks for being so young, Billy guessed, and Fingy chatted with a couple of hobos beside him. The sun dropped out of the sky and the fire warmed everyone. Billy kept quiet and listened to the talk. The men showed no interest in him, but whenever someone new entered the camp, the others looked over and asked the same questions. "So where'd you just come from?"

"Winnipeg," answered one.

"Toronto," said another.

"Any work there?"

"Nope. Nothing at all."

Billy began to worry. No work to be found anywhere. What chance did he have?

A couple of men got into idle chat about how to steal a chicken without raising the devil of a fuss. This way was best, said one, no that way, said the other, on and on till their voices rose in argument. Then the first fellow stood up.

"You grab it in one hand and put your ELBOW over its BACK! How d'ya think I *got* this chicken, anyhow, without gettin' caught! It didn't make no fuss before I WRUNG ITS NECK!"

He made a quick twisting motion with his hands to show how he'd finished off the chicken and that put a stop to the spat. Seemed he had stolen that bird in just such a way, plucked it, cleaned it, and they were all going to have a taste of it from the pot.

"Now we got a fine Mulligan!" announced Boss as he bent over to sniff at the meal. "Time to eat!"

He moved a worn camp chair closer to the fire and the men shoved over to make space for him. Billy leaned in to enjoy the fine fragrances of chicken, onions, corn and whatever else was cooking. Boss looked over at him in a meaningful way till he got the hint and took out his bread, broke some off and passed it around.

"He ain't got no tools," said one, jerking his head toward Billy.

Billy shook his head, feeling foolish for not having any spoon or fork. A man dished out some stew into a tin can and handed it to him. Another handed him a spoon.

"Keep them tools," he said. "You're gonna need 'em on the road."

Billy dug in, enjoying the thick meaty supper. When everything was eaten up, Fingy reached into his bindle and pulled out a Tootsie Roll that he passed along to him. In the light of the fire, Billy noticed Fingy's left hand had the tops of three fingers missing.

"What's your name, boy, and where you from?" Fingy asked him from across the campfire. The rest lay back, warm and fed and ready for a story or some entertainment. "Ain't got a home to go to?"

"Name's Mac. Mom and dad lost the farm," said Billy.

"Threw you out, eh?"

He nodded. It couldn't hurt to draw sympathy.

"How old are you? Ten?"

"Thirteen."

"You ain't been on the road long?" asked Fingy. He took a long drink from his canteen. "I'm headin' out on the midnight freight. You come along, I'll show you the ropes."

They lazed around the fire, idly talking as dusk came on and the first star hung in the sky. An old fellow took out his mouth organ and played a bouncing jig. Two men stood and stepped in time till one tripped on a stump and they fell about laughing. The music became more somber and the men sang along to a haunting tune, voices cracked except for a few good tenors among the crowd.

Don't bury me here on the lone prair-ee.

Boss snoozed in his chair, chin sunk on his chest.

An owl screeched, and the fire crackled and sparked. Talk around the fire turned to railway bulls and Billy sat up to listen.

"No mercy in 'em. No kindness," one man began, and others soon chimed in with wild stories. Some stood up and acted out the battles they'd had with this or that bull, always coming out smarter or stronger than their opponents. Huge bellows of laughter and wheezing coughs filled the night. But one fellow told his story in a quiet, bitter voice that hushed them all.

"Bastards aimed guns at us, frisked us," he began. "Told us, 'Strip off,' and they searched our rags and took half what we got hid in our pockets. My eighty dollars I got last summer pickin' apples, them bulls took forty! Had to give 'em forty bucks to ride the rails!"

Eighty bucks for picking apples! A good wage, thought Billy. Maybe when he reached the coast, he might try for that work.

"Nothin' we could do," the man continued, "standin' there

45

naked. Some got only two bucks to their name. They did better'n us, only paid a dollar."

Billy heard pain in the man's voice. That loss had hurt him bad, he bet, and stolen food out of the mouths of his family.

"Train passin' through at midnight," said Boss, waking up from his snooze. "Must be close on. Anyone catchin' out?"

No one answered, all of them too comfortable to move except Fingy, who stood up and slung his bindle over his shoulder. "I'm heading out." He turned to Billy. "Let's go, Mac. I'll show you the ropes."

Billy hesitated. Something about the man sent warning signals—that eagerness he'd shown to catch up with him on the road, and now this insistence they travel together. But he'd take a chance—keep on moving west.

He gathered his belongings and stepped out of the circle of firelight.

"Thanks for letting me sit in," he called.

The men muttered their good nights. The mouth organ's cheerful music played on and he left the camp with Fingy. If needed, he could always outrun him. That limp would surely slow him down.

—· **CHAPTER 5** ·—
FINGY

"How'd you lose them fingers?" Billy asked straight out as Fingy's uneven step kept pace with his own.

"Fell off a freight, my hand got too close." Fingy nursed his damaged hand with his good one for a moment as if the fingers had grown back and he was shielding them against another accident. "Lucky I still got a thumb and I can still grip. My knee got wrenched real bad. You heading to the coast?"

"I'm looking for work out there. Pickin' apples an' such."

"You'll do fine, kid like you. Look there," Fingy began to whisper. "Railway bulls. Watch out."

In the distance, men paced the line and shone lanterns up and down a freight train that sat silent on the track. The tendrils of a cold mist wrapped around the scene and formed halos of light around the station lamps. The two kept quiet and trod softly as Fingy led the way into the bushes alongside.

"Keep your head down while I have a look at the *sit-u-a-tion*." He crept away, then returned a few minutes later.

"All shut up tight," he whispered. "See that red light just come on? The train'll be leaving sooner or later. Catch a few winks, Mac, and when it gets going I'll wake you. We'll deck that train. You ever done that?"

Billy shook his head, no.

"It ain't hard. Just do what I do. You got a belt?"

"Yep, what for?"

"You'll find out," he said.

Billy sat down beside some bushes to keep hidden. His head sank onto his chest and he nodded off but awoke suddenly to Fingy's hand on his shoulder. He heard the huff of an engine. The train had begun to move forward at a walking pace.

"Let's go," hissed Fingy and ran with his lop-sided gait toward the track.

Billy heard a rustling sound to the left and right of him as a few more hobos stood up out of the scrub alongside. They spread out and raced toward the train to grab on wherever they could. Fingy turned and waited for Billy, then ran for a ladder and climbed upward to the roof of the train. Billy gripped a rung and swung up after him. At the top, he paused for a second to look around. Beams of glaring light swept along the deck.

"Get a move on!" hissed a hobo scrabbling up behind him.

Billy sprang from the ladder onto the roof and turned to look back.

"Get 'im!" a man shouted from below.

The hobo's fingers gripped the edge of the car and the top of his head appeared, eyes wide with fear. He gave a sudden yell of fright, jerked backward and dropped from view. Shadows danced in the beam of lantern light below and Billy heard thuds and howls of pain. The train gained speed and racketed along to leave the unlucky man behind.

Billy planted his feet on the long planks that ran down the middle of the boxcar roof. He stood for a moment to balance to the sway of the train, shivering with shock at the fate of that hobo. Up ahead, Fingy was taking quick steps along the walkway toward the next car.

"Let's go!" he called. "C'mon this way."

Fingy disappeared into the gloom ahead and Billy hurried to catch up. He reached a gap between the cars and discovered that the central catwalk extended a few inches over the edges of each car. He stepped easily across in spite of the cars' sideways motion. As he walked on, a warm breeze rushed at his face and whooshed in his ears. A red-hot cinder from the engine stung his cheek. He ducked his head and covered his face till at last he found Fingy sitting on the catwalk, his back turned against the smoke and heat.

"Sit down, Mac," he said, making room. "Don't worry about that 'bo. His luck ran out, but he'll be okay. They'll put him in the clink tonight, then run him out of town and he'll get the next catch out." He pulled out a Tootsie Roll from his bindle. "Here, have a snack. You did good back there. We make a fine team. We'll stick together." He yawned. "Time for some shut-eye. Here, tie yourself onto the deck so you don't roll off. Like this."

Fingy took off his belt, passed it under the plank on the catwalk and through one loop of his pants, then fastened the buckle, wrapped his jacket around himself and lay down with his bindle for a pillow.

Billy ate the candy, then tied himself on the same way. He prepared for a rough night on the train's back, but covered by his jacket, and with his bindle scrunched under his head, he fell asleep to the rhythmic rocking of the car.

Some hours later, he startled awake to the train's whistle. As Fingy snored beside him, Billy gazed upward and thrilled to see the heavens so brightly lit. He'd looked at the stars before, but never had he seen a night sky like the one on top of this freight train. He had the whole of it to himself. The Milky Way shimmered in the sky like a silver footpath. He saw shooting stars and found the Big Dipper that seemed to turn on its handle, putting on a show just for him.

He drifted off again and woke up to trace a flight of birds overhead, their shapes dark against the pale sky. As the train racketed along, he untied himself and sat up to gaze around.

Beside him, Fingy sat smoking a cigarette, and all along the cars, dozens of men stretched out lazing or sleeping. A thrill like an electric current shot through him—to be up high like this and all the land spread out below! Early morning sunlight glinted off the brown fields in flecks of gold. He felt a fellowship with the others as the train hurtled onward carrying them to places unknown. Just then on the opposite track, a freight train loaded with more hobos passed by, heading east. Billy and some others waved and the men waved lazily back. He looked for Ed among them, but each man looked identical, clothes ragged, and faces blackened from smoke and grease.

"Sleep good?" Fingy asked.

"Yeah. This train don't stop somewheres?"

"We're on a main line, no whistle stops."

Billy felt hunger pangs and shivered in the cool morning air.

Fingy handed him a Tootsie Roll. "Come on, we'll find a place out of the cold."

He stood and stretched, then walked back along the catwalk, moving from one car to the next. Billy ate the candy as he followed, stepping easily to the rhythm of the train.

They reached an open and low-sided car that carried tall metal containers. Fingy climbed halfway down a ladder on their car and jumped down into the flatcar. He looked up at Billy, his mouth curved in a faint smile.

"Come on down. Nice and warm right here." He pointed to a sheltered space near the containers. "No wind. Take a piss."

Billy climbed down and stepped onto the low edge of the flatcar, still holding the ladder for balance, then jumped in after him. But Fingy didn't stop and sit at this end. He walked on past the containers and disappeared around the side.

Billy stayed put, did his business over the side in the direction of the breeze, then sat and gazed at the view of fields along the route. The train slowed as it approached an incline. Fingy walked back to him and gestured toward the far end.

"Warmer back there. Let's go over that way."

"I'm fine right here."

"Come on, hon."

Fingy looked around him, then sat down and without warning his arms went around Billy, an eager look in his eyes and a half-smile on his face.

"Get away! Get off me!" Billy pushed the man away, struggled upright, reached for the ladder, and pulled himself onto the edge of the flatcar as he held onto a rung. Fingy grabbed at him, grasped him by the waist and lifted him back down.

Billy had heard about men who liked boys but until now had never had the bad luck to meet one. In disgust he struck out hard with his elbow in the man's face. But Fingy was too strong for him. Billy couldn't get away from those hands.

A sharp motion of the car pulled Fingy off balance. Billy kicked at him and the man's grip loosened, giving Billy a second to scramble away and grip the rung for balance. He pulled himself up onto the flatcar's edge and, desperate to escape, turned to face outward, gasping, his heart hammering, and the ground racing by. Too fast! Mac's voice in his head ... *"Never unload on the fly!"* He balanced there, swaying, staring ahead, trying to keep upright with both feet on the low wall of the flatcar and his hand still on the ladder.

"Don't jump! You're gonna get killed!" Fingy shouted.

But Billy was already in position. Better to risk some bruises than stay on that car. Knees bent, he took a breath, and leaped. He felt a swift bump to his head and the air left his lungs as he landed on his stomach, gasping like a fish out of water. He rolled along the ground moaning with pain. The stony surface bit into his flesh and the loose gravel slid beneath till he came to a stop, flat on his back. He could scarcely breathe and tried to force air into his heaving lungs.

But he was alive. And safe. The train clattered onward and away, and in the remaining quiet he heard the sound of running feet. Hands touched his arms and legs.

"Nothin' broke."

"Can you hear me?"

Billy's aching head could make no sense of anything. He

wiped at his eyes to get a better view and his hand came away bloody. He saw a tall boy standing over him wearing some kind of helmet, but a closer look revealed greased hair in spikes along the top of his head. The sides were shaved bald.

"He a friend of yours?" The boy gestured along the track. Billy turned his head to look and gasped in terror. Fingy must have jumped off to chase him. He now limped toward his bindle lying where he had flung it from the train.

"Perv," gasped Billy. "Don't let him near me! I was trying to get away. He's still after me."

The boy took out a silver whistle and blew it three times, loud and shrill. Billy heard shouts. A gang of kids came running toward them from every direction.

"Go chase off that perv, boys!" urged their leader, pointing at Fingy.

The boys swung away like a flock of birds pivoting in mid-flight and raced toward Fingy. They screamed threats and insults and some hurled stones. Fingy took one look at them, left his bindle where it had fallen and began to hurry away down the track.

Billy heard a voice in his ear. "You want me to kill 'im for ya?"

A small boy snatched a gun out of his pocket and stared down at him.

And that's how he met Tiny.

— · CHAPTER 6 · —
GOOSEBERRY PICKING

Tiny had yellow hair, looked much younger than Billy and couldn't have weighed more than fifty pounds. But with a gun in his hand he looked much bigger.

"Put it away, Tiny," the leader ordered.

The boy paid no attention. He levelled the gun, took aim at Fingy and walked toward the track, his pace quickening. As he reached the rails, some crows on the telephone wire above squawked a warning. Fingy kept moving, unaware of Tiny. The gang of boys stopped their taunts and fell back. At the sudden hush, Fingy turned to look around, saw the boy's gun pointing his way and uttered a croak as if his throat were full of marbles. Tiny kept the gun aimed, then in a flash he raised it skyward.

BANG.

A crow, perching on the telephone wire above, dropped like a stone.

Fingy yelled in panic and began to run.

The gang jeered and hollered insults. Tiny kept his sights on

Fingy until the man had moved around the bend and was out of view, then he blew on the barrel of his gun and stuck it in his waistband. He idly picked up a stem of grass to chew, and walked slowly back, the gang following behind. He sat down beside the campfire, eyes half-closed as if thinking hard about important matters.

The boys turned their attention away from Tiny and the dead crow. They stared at Billy.

Billy tried to get up, leaning on his good arm, but his knees buckled and he sat down quickly. His shoes were still on his feet but his bindle was gone. He'd left it on the train. The leader bent over him and lifted Billy's arm to look at his shoulder. Pain stabbed and Billy saw blood and a thick patch of skin that hung down where his shirt was ripped open. Seeing this, he heard a loud buzzing in his ears and his vision faded. A sharp voice in his ear made him swim up to awareness.

"Wake up, let's check you over."

The leader bent down and carefully helped him upright. With this sudden close-up view of him, Billy noticed the boy's face was deep brown from the sun, and each of his eyes showed a different colour, one green and the other blue. A small axe hung from his belt and alongside it, a beaded buckskin sheath held a hunting knife. As Billy was taking this in, he felt a hammer pound in his head and he swayed as if he were still on that freight train.

"I'm Spike," said the leader. "You'll get to know the rest of us soon enough. You sure hit the grit. We're gonna stitch you up. Boil the water, Shoestring. Get the sewing needle. Fix that rip."

"And the whisky?" answered a kid with a mop of untidy black hair that looked like it had never seen a comb.

"And the whisky."

Another boy ran over carrying a bindle and Spike took some interest in it. He unfastened the rope and drew out a bag of Tootsie Roll candies. Fingy's pack. Spike scattered the candies on the ground.

"Good work, fellas. Come get your reward."

About a dozen boys ran over to make a grab for the treats, uttering squeals and shouts at this windfall.

Shoestring returned with a bottle and rags. "Sit down on that rock there."

Billy lowered himself onto a rock beside the fire and Shoestring dabbed at his arm and cleaned away the blood, careful not to touch the raw part.

"You done this, before?" Billy asked, nervous.

Shoestring's eyes showed a glint of humour. He brushed a lock of hair away from his face and squinted through one eye as he threaded a sewing needle. "Seen it done lots of times. My mom was a nurse."

"Never lost anyone yet," added Spike.

The gang stood around, chewing their candy and interested in Shoestring's operation. Billy noticed their clothes were clean but didn't fit well, as though they'd raided cupboards and come up with pants and shirts a little too small or big for their size. They looked well fed and all were slim and strong.

And something else.

They made Billy think of his cat, Blackie. His dad had brought him home as a kitten, but after a month of living in the farmhouse, Blackie realized his own true nature and decided that domestic life was not for him. He went to live off the rats in the barn but Billy would sense him now and again or catch him lurking outside in the shadows. He had looked a darn sight better as a wild thing than ever he had when he belonged to Billy. Blackie knew exactly who he was and seemed to be saying he would never again get sucked into any house-cat nonsense.

These kids had that same look. *I don't belong to no one. Doing pretty good, thank you, and don't need you.*

"Doc's office is open for business," said Shoestring. "Here. Bite on this." He shoved a stick between Billy's teeth. "Hard. You're gonna need it."

What followed felt worse than the dog bite he'd had one time from a stray hanging around their farm. Shoestring poured some liquor over the wound. Billy flinched and gasped at the sting of it and was glad for that stick. Then Shoestring pushed the flap of skin back in place, held it with one hand and stitched with the other, a frown of concentration on his face. Billy watched the needle slip in and out through his skin just the way his mother darned his socks. He could feel that dog's teeth chewing at him all over again with every stitch. He almost cried out but stifled it. He saw their measuring looks, knew they were judging him, seeing what he was made of.

The boy wiped the blood off Billy's forehead, tied a strip of cloth around his head, and another piece around his arm. "Always lots of blood from head wounds," he said. "But don't worry, it's just a scratch."

"What we gonna do with him, Spike?" someone asked.

"We gonna let him in our tribe?" asked another.

"Come along for some grub," said Spike. "What's your name?"

"Mac."

"Well I got a better name for you—Rip! What do you think, boys?"

They agreed Rip was a fine name for someone with his skin half torn off, and some of them got a chuckle out of it. Billy began to get up but his head pounded, his vision blurred and next thing he knew, he was stretched out near a campfire under some blankets. He must have blacked out for a while. He heard voices and closed his eyes tight.

"You find any money on him?"

"In his shoes, likely. Check he's still got a pulse."

Hands tugged at his shoes but Billy stopped them with a kick. He opened his eyes.

A boy leaned over him, looking straight into his face. Tiny.

"He's awake."

Spike ambled over. "You passed out. You gonna live?" he asked him with no special interest.

Billy tried not to let out a groan as he sat up, feeling soreness in his shoulder and knees and a hammer in his head. He took a closer look around him. This jungle lay beside a dirt road that wound off among wild grass and bushes. To his right, the land rose up toward the track. On the other side, the waters of a lake shimmered in the morning sun. The camp looked neater than Boss's camp, with a place for everything and everything in its place—spaces to eat or sleep, or laze, a heap of bundles tied with string, and two firepits at a distance from each other. It seemed all packed and ready to move. Temporary.

Someone passed him a cup of soup to drink, then he dozed off again. He woke to darkness. Campfires flickered and he saw shadows in the firelight—kids coming and going, all busy with something or other. One of them helped him up and showed him a place to pee. He stumbled back to his blanket and the warmth of the fire, fell quickly into a dreamless sleep and awoke to sunshine and the chill morning air.

A skinny boy poked at the campfire nearby and lifted a steaming kettle. Some of his brown hair stuck out in tufts over a mostly shaven head, as if a clumsy barber had taken a rusty razor to it. He glanced at Billy. "You awake? Have some java." He poured water from the kettle into a can with holes at one end, holding it above a tin cup. Brown water dripped into the cup.

"They call me Sticky," he said and handed Billy the drink, along with a crust of bread to eat.

"Thanks, Sticky." Billy sipped the bitter drink, grateful for its warmth, and the bread helped fill a little of the hole in his stomach.

He glimpsed a few kids down by the lakeshore. Close by, a half-dozen boys lay all curled up together around the embers of another fire, fast asleep and covered in blankets.

A bird warbled. Billy looked around to see Spike walking toward them and blowing an intricate call on his whistle. The boys at the lake stopped what they were doing and straggled back into camp, Tiny among them. They carried bundles of wet clothes that they wrung out and hung on some bushes to dry. This job complete, the boys gathered around the fire, threw Billy some curious looks, and waited as Spike ambled over.

"Time for a powwow!" Spike sat down, drew his knife from its sheath and began to sharpen it on a stone. Billy watched him as the blade scraped, and waited anxiously to find out what they planned to do with him.

Spike fastened his gaze on Billy. "Rip, do you want to stay here a while? Or maybe you're thinking of jumping another freight."

"I might stay a while till my arm gets better, if it's okay."

"It's no trouble, long as you obey the rules and earn your keep. Fine job, Shoestring, on them stitches."

Shoestring nodded and looked proud.

"What're you good at?" Spike asked Billy. "You got any talents? Sing? Dance? Play a mouth organ?"

Billy shook his head. His mom always said he had a tin ear. She'd tried to teach him piano, but gave up after a month.

"So you gotta get by other ways." Spike finished sharpening the knife and slid it back inside its sheath. "If you ain't got no talent for singin' or playin' or dancin', you gotta get by on guts and charm and some pitying. You're gonna use your stitches and scabs and get lots of sympathy from the ladies in town. Shoestring'll show you how to milk that.

"We'll see how good you are at gooseberry pickin'," he continued. "You and Shoestring, go hit the stem, today. You need some new clothes, and Shoestring knows where to find 'em."

Billy looked down at his shirt and filthy pants. His shirt was bloody and ripped every which way to Sunday. His mother had sewn these clothes on her Singer. He was glad she couldn't see them now.

"Most important rule in this tribe—whatever you glaum or gooseberry comes straight to me. Got that?" It was an order. Spike held out his hand, palm up to illustrate the point.

He turned to Tiny. "Take Sticky with you and go glaum a chicken or something. And gimme your gat. Stay out of Biggar. They ain't forgot what you done last time and don't need to see you again for a while."

Tiny wore a large newsboy cap, and at these words he tugged it down to hide his eyes. Billy guessed he didn't agree with Spike because he shrugged and pressed his lips together before handing over the pistol tucked into his waistband. He slipped away down the track with Sticky. Billy watched them go. In the distance, a grain elevator stood tall and useless on that spoiled land and a clutch of houses lay scattered near the fields.

A few old hobos trudged down the road toward them and stopped to stare at the camp.

"Git!" Spike told them. "Nothin' here for you guys."

The men said good morning, and went on their way without any fuss.

"Bud and Tick, go glaum a blanket for Rip, here."

He tossed Fingy's bindle to Billy. "This'll do for you."

More orders went flying and each pair of boys got up on command to fetch this thing or that—a bucket, potatoes, some soap. Billy checked his bad arm. It pained him and looked a sight. The skin was ragged along the line of stitching, but it had scabbed up and looked clean enough. Shoestring came closer to check his work and nodded, satisfied.

"It's mending okay."

"Take the bandage off his head," ordered Spike. "A little blood showing is gonna get him some sympathy."

Shoestring unwrapped the bloody cloth and peered at Billy's wound. "I done a pretty good job! It's all nice and clean. Nice bruise and some good scabs. The ladies'll love that."

Billy stood up carefully and walked about, testing his legs. Spike tossed him an undershirt. "Might as well throw that shirt in the fire. Put this on."

Billy did so, watching the flames hiss and flare.

"So off you go," said Spike. "Take a walk with Shoestring and learn the ropes. Don't have to do nothing, for now. Just watch and learn."

Shoestring looked him over as if he didn't hold much hope for that. He shrugged. "Just follow along and do what I say."

He marched off across the tracks and Billy, much slower, followed him over some dusty fields. The wind blew the same way as back in Venn, a kind of steady moan that always drove his mom crazy. She would turn up the radio to drown out the sound. It didn't make any difference to that wind. It just blew harder.

Shoestring moved fast even though his sturdy leather shoes looked too big for him and he'd tied them around with different-sized strings and laces to keep them on tight. Maybe the boy hoped to grow into them, in time. He slowed at last to allow Billy to catch up, and they walked together along an unpaved road toward a few houses perched at the edge of a small town. Washing hung on lines in the backyards. One line held only women's clothing.

"Don't bother with that one," said Shoestring, dismissing it with a glance. "Her man's away. And even if we went begging, she likely won't open the door or give us nothin'. We gotta look for kids' clothes hanging, and toys in the yard. Those kinda folk'll take pity on us if we get caught."

"Caught for what?" Billy asked, though he had figured out what Shoestring was planning. Shoestring acted as if he hadn't heard, and stopped at another house to look at its laundry line with a family's worth of clothing pinned on to dry. But he muttered that the shirts and pants were already in rags, so he passed it by. They approached a brick house set back on the edge of a field, with a barn behind it, and spied a woman in the garden hanging laundry, her back to them. Shoestring ducked into a ditch at the side of the road, hidden by scrubby brush, and tugged Billy in after him, making shushing motions. They watched her peg on some boy's clothes that were in good shape.

She got to the bottom of her basket, rubbed her shoulder in a weary gesture, and went back inside.

"Time for some gooseberrying." Shoestring crept up out of the ditch. "You keep watch. She's likely checking her stew pot so we got a minute. Warn me if she comes out."

Whatever they called it, Billy knew it was plain stealing. Shoestring swung easily over the fence that bordered the garden, then stooped down to run behind the line of laundry. He passed by the flour sacks with holes for the head and arms, makeshift dresses for a girl, Billy guessed, and began to snatch boys' clothes from the line. He rolled them into a bundle and high-tailed it out of there, leaping the fence to streak down the road and away back to the camp. Billy watched from his perch in the ditch, shocked at how sudden it all happened.

He finally came to his senses. It was time for *him* to get moving, too. He began running behind, and his aches and pains twinged with each step.

When Spike saw their take, he seemed pleased enough. "Good haul." He hung the few damp shirts and pants on the bushes and turned to Billy. "When they're dry, you can pick out what you want."

Billy sank down by the fire. His stitches stabbed and a headache started up again. As he rested, Bud and Tick walked into camp, each carrying a bundle containing fresh eggs.

"Still waiting on the chicken," Spike said. "Where'd those boys get to?"

Sticky and Tiny turned up five minutes later with a dead hen, its neck hanging limply. This camp was real efficient, Billy thought.

The boys boiled some eggs and Billy ate one and drank some more coffee. When the stolen clothes had dried, he picked out some pants and a shirt from the bush and wondered about the family that had worn them, too poor to patch them up or find a missing button. And those flour sack dresses he'd seen on the washing line, with faded Quaker Oats stamps on them. Some little girl had to forget her pride to wear those.

He took off his own torn pants, no use now, and chose some work pants, a size too big, and worn at the knees. He tied them with his belt and rolled up the cuffs and they fit fine. But he felt sorry that some boy his age was out of luck, his clothing gone. The shirts were faded, with a couple of buttons lost, the collars threadbare. He swallowed his guilt. He had to earn his keep here and this was the only way to do it till he was well enough to move on. He put on a shirt, and was in business again.

But Spike wasn't done with him, yet.

"Okay, you and Shoestring are doing good together. You're going to hit the stem in Biggar. Hold onto this and Shoestring'll show you how to make it into a meal."

He handed them each a slice of grimy old bread.

Shoestring took off down the dirt track and as Billy hurried to catch up, he explained the trick as they walked along. Billy didn't like what he heard.

CHAPTER 7

WELCOME TO BIGGAR

The track widened into a dirt road among the fields, with wooden houses alongside. Trim front yards and painted fences showed folk were keeping up appearances in spite of hard times. At a crossroads, signs pointed to places north and south, but one sign stood out with bold letters painted in black:

NEW YORK IS BIG

BUT THIS IS

BIGGAR

POPULATION 1,907

They turned onto Biggar's wide main street lined with stores, an important looking town hall fronted with two pillars, and a real library, much grander than the library in Venn. That one had just a shelf of books in the grocery store while this must have thousands.

"Must be a ton of books in there," said Billy. "I'd sure like to see them."

But Shoestring was eyeing the main street. "Can't do it. We got stuff to do."

The shops that lined the street were mostly empty and closed up tight, some with boards nailed over the windows. Across from the library stood a post office and a barber shop. Here, men leaned against the wall while others sat on a bench in front. Not hobos, Billy saw. More respectable. Local men out of work, but still making a go of it somehow, and passing the long day with chitchat.

Shoestring sent him on to walk past them and get to the top of Main where all the houses started. "I'm staying down this end. Meet me back here when you're done. Don't get into trouble."

As Billy passed the group, one of the men called out to him. "Where you from?"

"Venn."

"How're folk doing in Venn? Hard going?"

"My dad lost his farm." Billy guessed the fellow was going through the same troubles or he wouldn't be here on this street corner to pass the time. The man nodded and smiled at him in a kindly way. "What happened to you, son? You get hurt?"

"Fell off a freight train."

He shook his head slowly. "You be careful, young fella. Don't take chances."

This next part was going to be tough and Billy almost threw

that bread away, deciding he'd pretend the trick didn't work. Shoestring was down the block but Billy could see him glancing his way now and again, keeping an eye on him, so he had to see it through.

He found the little house with the gate that Shoestring had described. There was a mark chalked on it, placed there by Spike's gang to show a kind lady lived here.

Lace curtains hung at the windows and a few steps led up to the front door. Billy hesitated. Walking through that gate meant he was just like one of them, tricking and stealing. "I'll do it this once," he thought. "Just till I can get on my way." He went in at the gate, dropped his piece of bread on the steps the way Shoestring had explained, knocked and hurried back to stand on the sidewalk. A woman opened the door and peered out. She wore a blue housedress and had a head of curly greying hair. Shoestring had told him how to get a woman on your side, flatter them that they look so young.

"Good day, miss, is your mother at home?"

"What is it?"

"Please, ma'am—I see you got a piece of bread on your step. Can I have it? Maybe you got another so's I can make a sandwich?"

71

She looked down at the bread, and her eyes told him she knew his trick.

"How old are you, son?" she asked. "What happened to your face? You fall off a freight train? You can't be more'n twelve. Don't you have a home?"

He put on a sad face. "No, ma'am. Mom and dad can't take care of me. Told me to go take care of myself."

"You come inside," she said. "I'm going to make you a lunch."

Shoestring had told him to first say no thank you, act polite and respectful.

"No, thank you ma'am. I'll just take this bread along with me. I don't want to dirty your rugs."

"You come on in this minute," she smiled. "Don't worry about that." He stepped along the hallway and into her sparkling clean kitchen and a young girl came in and sat down at the table. She smiled and glanced at him in a shy manner. To Billy, it seemed she was pink all over—from her cheeks and hair ribbon to a frilled pink apron tied over her crisp white dress.

"This is my granddaughter, Katie, come to stay a while. And my name's Mrs. Cooper." The woman opened cupboard doors as she chatted. She reminded Billy of a magpie picking up this and that item, her eyes bright and curious. She told him about Biggar and what a good little town it was. Billy felt Katie watching him, but whenever he glanced at her, she looked somewhere else and her cheeks flushed pink.

"Let's see," said her grandmother as she opened the bread box. "I just baked this bread yesterday, nice and fresh, 'less you want me to use that old piece of bread on the steps."

Billy hung his head, but she smiled. "I guess you're having a hard time of it and have to do whatever you can for your next meal. I bet you got some stories to tell."

She opened a cupboard door and Billy saw nothing in it but one can of sardines.

"You ain't got much," Billy blurted. "Sure you can spare it?"

"It's shopping day," she answered. "We always get supplies today. Not to worry." She sliced some bread, made him a sandwich, and had him sit down at the table to eat it. She wrapped another sandwich to take along with him. "One for the road," she said with a smile. "Now you gotta earn your lunch. Tell us about your travels. What's it like jumping on trains without a ticket?"

Katie had been quiet until now, but at the mention of the rails, she leaned forward in her seat, her cheeks flushed a deeper pink with excitement.

"It's a great life!" he began between bites, finishing off the sandwich and enjoying the attention. "And dangerous, too. I've had railway bulls chasing me, but I always outrun 'em. One time they almost got me, grabbed my shirt when I was climbing a ladder, but I was too quick for 'em and got away along the deck. Sleeping up there, the sky above full of stars, why it's just swell to watch them shooting stars, and all the twinkle up there. And the food ain't bad. One time, a waitress gave me a full meal and a dollar besides, all free. I tell you, riding the rails is the best adventure a man can ever have!"

He figured telling a few lies would be good entertainment for them, especially Katie with her neat, pressed clothes and quiet life. He bet she never got out anywhere, poor kid.

"I get to see the country from the top of a freight, and I plan to get to the Pacific Ocean, and travel to China on a ship!" He had never dreamed of such a thing, but here in the warm kitchen with a friendly audience, anything seemed possible.

"You're so brave," Katie murmured. "Isn't he, Gran?"

"Yes. It's an adventurous life," agreed Mrs. Cooper. "What do you want to be when you're older?"

"A train engineer," he stated proudly. "Or a ship's captain," he invented, "... so I can keep on travelling." He realized that was true. To have a job that took him to far-off places would be perfect. He had finished his sandwich and remembered Shoestring was waiting at the other end of town. "I'd best be on my way, now. Thank you, ma'am, for your kind hospitality."

"Wait a minute," said the lady. She went to the hall closet, took out a wool jacket, and held it out to him. "You'll need this.

Nights will get cold soon enough. My husband's in the grave," she gave a wry smile, "and doesn't need it now."

He remembered Shoestring's instructions. "Once you get inside, take whatever she gives you, and more when she's got her back turned." He hesitated, but at the lady's urging, he tried it on. It was a size too big, but warm.

"Thanks, Mrs. Cooper," he said, feeling low at taking anything from her. "You're a kind lady and I won't forget it."

"And take this quarter," she answered and offered him the coin. He shook his head but to no avail. She took hold of his hand and placed it in his palm.

He said goodbye to them at the door, and glanced back as he walked along. Katie still lingered at the doorway and he threw her a parting wave, then met up with Shoestring again at the end of the street. The boy held a full sack and nodded approval at the jacket.

"That'll fit Spike. He'll be happy with it. And I glaumed some spuds."

Shoestring unwrapped the extra sardine sandwich and ate it as they walked along back to camp.

"How long has Spike bossed your jungle?" Billy asked, curious about Spike's set-up.

"We don't call us that. We call us a tribe," Shoestring answered. He explained that Spike was the Chief, and they'd all been travelling together for a long time, going on a year, and planning to ride the rails down south this winter to stay warm. They might soon hop a train and head on down the line.

"We pack up and move camp now and then. People start to notice us, and it's time to leave."

"I'm planning on picking apples out west," Billy said, just so Shoestring would know he was set to move on.

"You got folk there?"

"Nah. I gotta make some money to send home. You got any folk somewhere?"

"My mom died," said Shoestring. "Dad already left us. I didn't want to go to some orphans' home so I ran. Got lucky when I got in with Spike. How's your arm?"

"You did a good job on it," said Billy. "It itches but it feels fine."

"Wait another day till them stitches come out. You're better off sticking with us. Out there, you got pervs, killers, all kinds. Not so easy."

"I like going on my own steam," he said. *I don't like Spike's ways*, he thought.

But he kept that to himself.

Back at camp, Spike sat by the campfire, whittling as usual. The blade caught the late afternoon sun. Billy figured he kept the knife in view in case anyone had doubts about who was boss of this tribe. Nearby, some boys played a quiet game of tag. The night boys were just beginning to wake up after they had slept the day away.

Shoestring laid down the sack of potatoes, and Billy held out the widow's gift.

"I got a jacket."

Spike gave the jacket an assessing look and reached out to touch its fine wool tweed and the leather-covered buttons.

"A little fancy for the likes of us, ain't it?" he said. "Might fetch a dollar." He tested the blade of his knife against his finger, and put it away, satisfied. He held out his hand, palm up. "Coins?"

Billy gave him the quarter.

"That all you got? You could do better." Spike took the jacket and his long fingers slid into its pockets. The silk lining revealed a hidden pocket and he pulled out a folded bill.

"A tenner. Good haul." He slipped the bill into the leather pouch hanging from his belt.

Billy knew Mrs. Cooper could have used that extra ten. He felt angry with Spike, and with himself, too. This way of living put a sour taste in his mouth.

Spike must have caught his expression. "You plannin' on stayin' around?"

"Plannin' to catch out soon," said Billy. "Get on my way. I'm headin' west. Soon as my arm's good, I can hop a train."

He glanced at the stitches on his arm. The wound was healing neatly with just a small pucker across the skin. The cut on his face had scabbed, and his headaches had stopped. He could hardly wait to be on his way.

CHAPTER 8

CHAUTAUQUA

"Rip, go along with Tiny today," Spike ordered the next morning. He sat near the campfire, grooming his hair upward, his long fingers spreading grease through the strands.

Billy had slept deeply last night and woken up feeling back to his normal self, his headache gone. He'd eaten a good breakfast of fried eggs and ham, and wondered what this day would bring. He sat with the day boys around the campfire, as Spike gave them their orders for the morning's work. Tiny had ambled up with a full sack hoisted over his shoulder, the brim of his hat tilted low to hide his eyes. He dumped the sack in front of Spike. Ears of corn tumbled out.

Spike nodded his approval at Tiny's haul. "You can learn a lot about glauming from Tiny," he told Billy. "He's a natural. You two can do a brothers act. The ladies'll love it." He jerked his chin at Tiny. "So meet your new big brother. Shoestring's taught Rip a few things but he can use some more educating."

Tiny shot a look at him and Billy saw a flash of derision.

"Tiny's our best actor. Let's practise awhile. Here's the scene, Rip," said Spike, leaning back on his elbows. "Say you're stemming in town. You knock on a door, a lady opens it and right away, you smell something real good cooking that makes you drool. You sure want some of that. How will you get it?"

Tiny and Spike waited for his answer as Billy gave it some thought.

"You got a job I can do for you?" Billy suggested.

Tiny snorted.

"You wanna end up breaking your back chopping firewood?" said Spike. "Mucking the barn for a few pennies? Now, Tiny here has a better system. Show him, Tiny."

Tiny took off his cap and held it over his heart. His face took on a soulful expression and his eyes got bigger and rounder as he looked at Billy. "Ma'am, you must be a *wonderful* cook. That smells just like my mother's cooking!" His blue eyes turned sad, as if he were remembering something he'd rather forget.

Billy was already convinced by Tiny's story. If *he* were that hungry but had just one sandwich left in all the world, he would give it up to Tiny, his story was that believable. But Tiny wasn't finished with him. He paused for a beat, looked down, then turned his gaze full on Billy, and wham, he hit it home—"... before she went and died, and left me all alone." He let out a sob, ducked his head and wiped away real tears with his fist.

"See? Perfect! That's how it's done!" Spike applauded. "Give 'em compliments and get their sympathy." He turned back to Billy. "Now, Rip, suppose you knock on a door, a man opens it and he looks mean as hell. What're you gonna say?"

Tiny crossed his arms and stared at Billy, waiting. Billy gave up and looked to him for help. The boy took his cue. He gazed downward, his fingers worried at the cap in his hand, turning and twisting it this way and that. Billy watched, fascinated as he lifted his head, his expression a picture of misery and worry. Another tear welled up and he wiped it away.

"Sorry to trouble you, sir," he said, voice wavering. "My dad died and Mom told me I have to get out 'cause we lost everything. I've just been on the road a little while. I haven't et today. Do you know a place I could get a little something?"

All finished, he stood up straight and the sadness emptied out of his face like a fast-leaking bucket.

"Tiny's a class actor," Spike said. "Best we got. Think you can teach Rip, here?"

Tiny raised his eyes skyward to show there was no hope for Billy. He shoved his cap back on his head.

Spike stared at Billy. "You're gonna need a cap, too," he said. "Sticky, go fetch me one from the sack over there."

Sticky jogged over to the sleeping area and bent to rummage in one of the bundles. He drew out a flat cap and brought it over.

"Caps are good for all kinds of things," said Spike, as he pushed down his hair and placed the cap on his own head. He stood up to demonstrate. "You saw Tiny using it a couple ways. And you can tip it like this when you meet a lady." He gave a quick nod as he touched the brim with his forefinger to demonstrate. "Or you can take it right off your head to show respect." He removed it with a sweeping gesture and gave a brief bow. "And you can beg for coins like this." He ducked his head as he thrust the upturned cap toward Billy. "So watch and learn from Tiny," he said, reaching up to pat his spiked hair into place as he handed Billy the cap. "Now, light out, you two. Tiny, stay out of Biggar."

Tiny stood up from the fire and stretched, then gave Billy a look and jerked his chin at the tracks. He walked off along the rails without a backward glance. Billy followed. They trod along the ties and gravel, *step, crunch, step, crunch,* Billy a few steps behind as Tiny whistled and hummed a tune. After a while of step and crunch and whistling and humming, he threw some words back at Billy.

"You plannin' on stayin' in our tribe?"

"I'm headin' west, soon as my stitches come out. How long you been with them?"

"I never count. Spike always says we only got today."

Tiny waved his cap to shoo away some black flies. Billy tried to guess the boy's age. His face was brown as a walnut from the sun, and his hair a pale bleached yellow. Maybe ten years old, he figured, except he must have seen a lot of trouble. It showed on his face. His forehead was wrinkled as if he'd spent a long time weighing up hard choices.

Instead of avoiding Biggar as Spike had ordered, Tiny led them straight to it. At the signpost, they noticed some bustle down Main Street. A crowd of town folk had gathered, talking together. All of a sudden, people began to wave their arms and jump about, calling out, "Welcome! Welcome to Biggar!"

For a moment, Billy thought the crowd was calling to him and Tiny, but the *putt putt putt* of motors purred behind them. He turned to see two sleek Model A's approaching, one coloured a country green, the other, a polished black, both with brass fixtures that flashed in the sun. Inside the open-topped cars sat elegant ladies with fancy hats, and smart gentlemen in good suits.

A group of children rushed up and in unison they chanted a rhyme.

> "C-H-A-U This is how you spell it!
>
> C-H-A-U Listen to us yell it!
>
> Chautauqua! Chautauqua! CHAUTAUQUA!"

The car slowed as the passengers waved and smiled their greetings. Billy saw women's slim hands with painted nails and men's thick hairy hands, all sparkling with gaudy rings and bracelets. The crowd made way for them, then thronged behind, smiling and cheering all the way down the main street. Tiny marched right past the Biggar sign and into town, a spring in his step.

Billy ran to catch up. "Spike said don't come here."

"He ain't gonna find out," Tiny answered. "Least, he better not." He frowned at Billy and walked onward to follow the small parade.

The cars stopped at a grassy park at the end of Main Street where a stage rested on oil drums. Around it, men struggled with big sheets of brown canvas, while others pounded stakes into the ground. One important-looking man in shirtsleeves studied a large sheet of paper as he shouted instructions and waved his arms at the workers.

Tiny nudged Billy and gestured to a poster nailed to a lamp post at the street corner. They walked over to read it.

Biggar's Annual Chautauqua Tent Show

Eighty Entertainments!

Free Opening Show Tonight!

"Says it's free. I'm hangin' around," said Tiny. "I hear these fellows are the cat's pyjamas. They do plays and stuff. Maybe they got a part for me."

The two watched as workers tied flapping canvas pieces to the poles, tightened them, and the man with the blueprints walked around, checking this and that pole. When all the pieces were assembled into one very large tent, he nodded in approval, satisfied it wouldn't tumble down.

Tiny strolled around the big tent toward some smaller ones at its rear. Through the canvas opening of the nearest one, Billy caught sight of a beautiful lady wearing a white feather boa. She put on her lipstick with the aid of a hand mirror.

Beside her stood a tall gentleman in a top hat and wearing a tailored suit. He waved his arms about and cleared his throat as if about to say something very important. After a few throat noises and some more arm waving, he began to speak in a deep bass voice.

"Ladies and Gentlemen, you may be astonished to learn ..."

He stopped for more throat clearing. Billy waited with some impatience, hoping to find out what was so astonishing, but the man only repeated the same words as before and cleared his throat again.

Billy turned to Tiny, but the boy had gone off somewhere, so he wandered back onto Main Street. It seemed the whole town had gathered there. Country folk had ridden in from neighbouring farms and tied their horses and wagons to posts along the road. Billy saw a couple of Bennett buggies—broken-down cars hitched to horses because the owners could not afford gas to run them. Among the crowd, he glimpsed Katie with her grandmother walking along, pausing to chat with people along the way. He moved in the opposite direction and spied Tiny waiting in line at the lemonade stand among laughing and chattering townsfolk. Small children tugged at their parents' sleeves and asked for nickels to buy ice cream.

Tiny paid for his drink and carried the cup past Billy, his eyes focused on keeping it steady and not spilling a drop. He was heading back to the smaller tent and Billy followed, curious.

"Good afternoon, Miss," Tiny called through the tent flap.

Billy peeked inside and caught a glimpse of the lady, brushing her fine chestnut hair. The gentleman sat in front of a table mirror with a towel around his neck, applying a tan colour to his face from a bottle, his top hat beside him on the floor.

"I brought you some lemonade in case you're thirsty," Tiny said.

The woman looked up in a distracted way, but at sight of him she put on a big smile, laid down her brush and held out her hand to welcome him inside.

"Aren't you sweet! Come on in and tell me all about yourself, sweetheart. What do they call you?"

Tiny marched right in. Billy tried to hear the conversation, but the noise of the crowds around him drowned out their voices. Someone played a harmonica nearby, but over its cheerful tunes, he could hear snatches of the lady's soft, silvery voice as she laughed at something Tiny said.

Spike was right. Tiny sure could turn on the charm!

He felt drawn to the Model A's he'd seen parked outside the hotel. He left Tiny to whatever trick he was playing, and walked back through the crowds to take a closer look. There they stood, the most beautiful cars he'd ever seen. He moved closer to the green car and reached out to touch its hood ornament, a silver bird in flight, wings outspread.

"Get back, kid!" said a fellow nearby. He wore a black cap with a crest. "Keep your grubby fingers off. Just cleaned them cars."

Billy stepped away but got an eyeful of those fine soft leather seats, the polished brass and shining wheel spokes. The rims were the colour of the cream from his dad's milk cows. He imagined himself driving one of these fancy cars all the way to the west coast at top speed, sixty miles an hour. He would reach the ocean in no time, then drive it right back home to show his mom and dad. He could just see the looks on their faces—all lit up in amazement.

All of a sudden, Tiny appeared at his side. The outline of a red lipstick kiss decorated his cheek, and his face shone with excitement.

"She plant one on you?" Billy asked, feeling admiration for the boy. Tiny looked proud but didn't answer. He rubbed at the spot to wipe it off.

"Let's beat it. We're supposed to be glaumin'."

They left the crowds behind and took the dirt road toward a farm they could see in the distance.

As they walked, Tiny poured out a cascade of words about the lady in the tent. It seemed to Billy that once he got started, there was no stopping the flow.

"Miss Janet's a real doll. She says I gotta come up on stage with her and act in the play and bring her a drink. She'll give me twenty-five cents."

"That's swell! How'd you get that part?"

"Hell, I'm an actor. Miss Janet could tell right away. Us actors know each other on sight. I acted the scene about my mother dying and turned on all the taps. I was so good, Miss Janet about swooned."

Tiny could bring on the phony tears but Billy wondered if his story was all true.

"Your mother really dead?" he ventured.

"Dead to me," he answered, then shut his mouth in a tight line. It seemed to Billy as if he'd stacked bricks around that subject and piled on cement, too. So he really must be a fine actor, crying tears like that for someone he didn't care for.

They passed the Biggar sign, then kept walking a mile or so toward the farmhouse that stood in bleak contrast against the blue sky. Billy saw the dust piled up around it, heaped against the walls and fences. A fine cloud of it rose around his ankles as he walked along. This could have been his own family's farm, all its paint scoured away by dust storms, the wind always snatching at the ground to hurl dust around like a spoiled kid having a tantrum.

A winding track led up to a barn. Billy could see places where swarms of grasshoppers had been chewing. A broom leaned against a wall, its bristles eaten away. A rake stood alongside, its wooden handle chewed up by hoppers hungry for the salt from sweaty palms.

He shivered as he remembered the first time he'd seen that dark cloud—millions of them, flying toward their farm. He'd looked at the swarming shape-shifting cloud through a piece of amber glass, better able to pick out separate insects, and frightened they were about to descend. They hadn't that day, but another storm of hoppers landed a week later and chewed up their wheat and even the horses' leather harnesses. They'd marked their farm walls with splatters and splashes of brown grease from smacking into walls and windows. His mom just gave up when that happened. No use in trying to fight it anymore.

Tiny tried the farmhouse door, but it was shut tight. The washing line was empty of laundry.

"They're all in town, I bet," said Tiny.

Or gave up and moved away, like Mom and Dad, thought Billy and felt a wisp of sadness brush his heart for all their losses.

89

"Good day for glauming with everyone out." Tiny picked up a rock to aim at the kitchen window.

Billy put out a hand to stop him. "Nothin' here, and I'm not robbing them. They don't have nothin' anyway."

Tiny did not look convinced, so Billy tried a different tactic.

"Do whatever you want. I'm going back to town. You see them Model A's? And maybe Miss Janet's got a part for me, too." As he turned and walked away, he heard Tiny's rock hit the ground. His plan had worked.

"You ain't got the talent," Tiny said, hurrying after him.

Back in town, the jostling crowd had grown even larger. People surrounded a pair of jugglers tossing five balls into the air, and listened to an accordion player. A posted sign stated that a free sample show would begin in the tent at five o'clock. Tiny figured they had a few hours to wait, but he led the way to the entrance of the big tent, its flaps closed up tight.

"We gotta be first in line so I can get a seat up front for when Miss Janet wants me on stage," he explained and sat down on the ground. "We can take turns sitting here so no one busts in front."

Billy held their places while Tiny went to buy some sausages on a bun and some lemonade for them. The two took turns, one held the spot while the other drifted around town to watch the fun.

Some pushy moms and dads sat down at the entrance, and tried to shove their kids in front of the boys, but Tiny pushed them right back. A few hours later, a hand from inside the tent reached out to pull back the flap. Billy and Tiny jumped up and began to charge inside but bumped straight into a bossy frowning man at the entrance. He towered over them and tried to push them back out.

"Step back. Get in line!"

They dodged around him and ran into the tent to get a place right at the front. Those in line behind ran in too, and everyone sat down on the grass floor, close to the stage. Soon, the tent was buzzing with an audience that filled the tent from front to back.

Tiny stared up at the blue velvet curtains and looked tight with impatience to see them sweep open. At last, when it seemed the tent had filled to the rafters, the curtains opened, and the audience hooted and clapped and whistled.

An announcer waited for silence.

"Ladies and gentlemen. Boys and girls. It is my pleasure to introduce His Worship, Mayor Boyd."

The Mayor of Biggar wore a gold chain with a medal that hung down and rested on his rotund stomach. He started a speech about his fine town and how proud he was to live here. The crowd listened politely, but as the talk rambled on and on, people began a steady clap, clap, clap, till at last the mayor got the message, bowed to them and left the stage. An announcer stepped forward.

"Ladies and Gentlemen, I present to you the wise and worldly, the fascinating and famous ... Julius Caesar!"

Tiny squirmed with impatience, waiting for Miss Janet's turn. The speechy man they'd seen practising, now wore his top hat and a black cape with a red lining that flashed when he swished it around. He stepped up and began.

"Ladies and Gentlemen, you will be astonished to learn ..." he paused, and now Billy leaned forward, eager to hear the rest of it. "... that a few hundred years ago, boys wore dresses, and women's skirts were so wide that their wearers became wedged in doorways!"

He gestured to robes and clothes that hung on stands behind him, in all the colours of the rainbow. "Do I have a volunteer to model this finely woven shawl from the eighteenth century?" he called, holding up a deep blue shawl with fine stitching.

"Me! I'll come up," called a lady and she hustled forward. A farmer's wife, she wore a drab grey dress sewn up with patches here and there.

The crowd made way for her and Julius helped her up on stage and told a lively story about the soft woven shawl as he draped it around her shoulders. She twirled about, a sparkle in her eyes as if she were no longer a farmer's wife but a queen or duchess.

More volunteers sprang onto the stage to model coats and capes, and in rich syrupy tones, Julius related a fascinating story about each one. He ended his lecture to cheers and Billy knew he wouldn't mind listening to the whole talk all over again, it was that good. The curtains closed and an expectant hush followed. Tiny sat up straight, eyes glued to the stage. The announcer came out to introduce the next act, a small scene from a play they'd be performing tomorrow, at the cost of ten cents for a ticket.

"We present the glamorous, the beautiful, the gifted, Miss Janet Walker!"

The curtains opened to Miss Janet, lounging on a divan and fanning herself with a lace fan.

"This your part?" Billy whispered, but Tiny was already gone from his side and jumping up onto the stage. He disappeared around the side curtain.

"Too, too hot," Miss Janet sighed in exasperation. "Where is my cocktail? It's past three o'clock." She rang a little silver bell on a side table, fanned herself, and rang the bell again. Billy held his breath, waiting.

Tiny pranced in, nose in the air, wearing a black waistcoat, and holding a drink on a silver tray. He placed the glass on a side table, little finger raised, then bowed quickly from the waist, three times.

"It's about time!" complained Miss Janet. "I've been ringing the bell for simply ages!"

"Don't cry tears over it, Madam," said Tiny, in a loud, clear voice. He turned to the audience, and gave them a big wink, "... 'cause that drink's already been watered down!"

He mimed drinking from a bottle and the crowd loved it. They laughed and applauded, and Tiny strutted around the stage to soak up the attention, then disappeared into the wings. An actor who played Miss Janet's fiancé walked on, and during their lines, Billy saw Tiny come back and sit down on the stage at its very edge to get a close-up view. With his eyes fastened on Miss Janet, he seemed all wrapped up in the story and sat as still as a piece of stage furniture. He leaned against the thick velvet curtain as the two actors began an argument. At the end of the scene they made up and kissed. The kiss went on for a long time and they kept looking over at the curtain. Billy guessed they were waiting for it to close so they could finish kissing and leave the stage. A stagehand came out in front to investigate and discovered that Tiny was sitting on a piece of the curtain. He shoved him out of the way and it closed at last.

What a night! Billy thought that was the best acting he'd ever seen, even though he'd never seen a play before, except for the Christmas pageant his school put on last year. He followed the crowd out of the tent and looked around for Tiny. The sun was setting and they would be late back to camp with nothing to show for their day. But it had been worth it for all the fun he'd had.

He headed to the dressing tent and stuck his head around the flap. In the lamplight, he found Tiny at Miss Janet's feet, gazing up at her, as she cooed over him like a mother pigeon.

"Here's a dollar," Miss Janet said and handed him a bill. "You're a natural, so talented. And we can use you again, tomorrow night." She noticed Billy. "Who's this young man?"

Billy smiled and tipped his hat the way Spike had shown him.

"That's Jake," Tiny invented.

"Come to take my brother home, Miss," Billy said.

"Come in. Are you an actor, too, like your brother Charles?"

"He's not bad," said Tiny. "I've been teaching him."

Billy heard heavy steps behind him, and a commotion of gruff voices. He peeked out through the flap. A crowd of men were stomping up toward the tent, faces like thunder.

"Miss Janet, you decent?" a voice growled. "You got that thievin' kid in there?"

Tiny jumped up in alarm. Billy had never seen fear written on Tiny's face but he saw it now. "Don't let 'em in!" he hissed to Billy. He crouched back down and took a sudden dive under the back canvas wall, till all Billy could see of him was his rump as he scrabbled out.

"Just give me a second," called Miss Janet, waving at Billy to leave the same way, her eyes round with surprise.

Billy didn't waste a minute. He wriggled under the canvas and ran as fast as he could, dodging this way and that through the crowds till he had put some distance between himself and those men. Spike had warned Tiny to stay out of Biggar. Whatever he had done, it was enough to stir people up.

Billy reached the edge of town and walked quickly on until the noise and bustle were behind him. Crickets began to sing in the grass, then just as suddenly stopped. A hush descended on the endless prairie land, an expectant silence as if something hidden waited in the tall grasses. A patch of grass began swaying and Billy jumped, startled. Tiny popped up beside him out of the shadows. "Them men still after me?"

"I guess. Miss Janet held 'em back so I could get away, too," said Billy. "What did you do to 'em? They were pretty mad."

Tiny ignored the question, and walked along in front, no hurry to his step. A distant train whistle sang a warning note.

"When you catching out?" Tiny asked.

"A couple of days. Shoestring is gonna cut my stitches off, and I want to get on my way."

"Let's go back in town tomorrow night. After the show, I'm gonna bust out with you, tag along," he said. "But I'm goin' back and act my part again, maybe get a better one."

"You crazy? Those men ..."

"They can't catch me," he scoffed. "And I'm plannin' to meet up with Miss Janet in Vancouver and do another show. She's leaving Sunday for the next go-round."

"She's a dish! She ask you along?"

"She don't know about it yet. I can do odd jobs, move up the line, get a swell acting part."

"Hot damn, you were good up there! You're just a natural," Billy said.

"I know it."

Billy wondered if Spike would stop him leaving. Tiny was so good at glauming, probably the best in the whole tribe. "You think Spike's gonna let you go?"

"It ain't Spike's business. Tomorrow night, get ready to fly the coop when they're all sleepin'. We'll meet up by the track after the show."

"How're you gonna do the play without getting caught?"

They were approaching the edge of the camp. "Ssh! Talk about it later," Tiny hissed.

All was quiet, and a few boys dozed around the flickering fire. The night gang had already left to perform their stealing and begging chores under cover of darkness.

This was how the tribe worked, guessed Billy, they glaumed around the clock till they milked a town dry, then moved on before people caught on to them. It must be time to break camp soon, the way Tiny drew unwanted attention.

A figure loomed up ahead. Shoestring.

"Where's Spike?" Tiny asked.

"Went off somewhere with the gang. You're kinda late back. Spike's mad as a bull. Where you been?"

"Nowhere special." Tiny yawned and stretched. "Time to hit the sack."

Billy felt relieved he would not have to explain to Spike what they had been up to. He crawled under his blanket near the campfire, and slid off to sleep. A freight train rumbled by and he was soon dreaming that he lay on its deck as the stars whirled above and put on a show.

—· **CHAPTER 9** ·—

RUN!

"Where'd you boys get to last night?" Spike glared at them. "Where's the take?"

Billy gulped his coffee, playing for time. He could hear the day boys splashing in the lake. The rest of the gang lay near the campfire, fast asleep after a hard night's work.

"We got chased off a farm," said Tiny. He gave a tug at his newsboy cap to cover his eyes. "Farmer ran out with a shotgun, so we took off. Didn't have no luck. Everybody was in town for the show. Bad day for glauming."

"Could've picked some pockets," said Spike. He took out his knife and began to whittle a stick.

"I'm supposed to stay clear of town, like you said."

"But you went anyway," said Spike, meaningfully. "Enjoy the show?" He didn't wait for an answer. "You broke curfew. Don't do it again. Boys and me had a powwow last night. We're packing up in a couple of days, heading west. You coming along, Rip?" he asked.

Billy tried to catch Tiny's eye, but he had turned his back to poke at the fire.

"Sure," said Billy. He figured if he and Tiny were leaving tonight, he'd better just keep quiet and wait for Tiny to take the lead.

"Good, then," said Spike, his eyes moving from Tiny to Billy, and back again. Billy felt a cold shiver as he watched the boy whittle that stick till it was sharp and pointy.

"So, Tiny. You and Sticky'll be partners today. And stay out of town. Sticky, keep an eye on him. And Rip, you go along with Shoestring. The larder's getting empty. Go glaum some eggs. But take a look at his arm, Shoestring."

Shoestring poked at Billy's injury, then fetched some scissors. "The stitches can come out," he said. "Won't hurt." He snipped at the threads and Billy felt only a slight discomfort at each tug. The wound had healed fine with just a little pucker in one place, and a tiny scar.

Billy hoped for a quiet word with Tiny about their plans, but he and Sticky were already walking away along the track. There was nothing for it but to go into town with Shoestring for the day.

"Watch out for the cops in town," Shoestring said as they walked along the road. "They'll be out looking for pickpockets." He stooped to tighten the strings on one of his shoes. "If you run into one, get close to a family with kids, and say something like, 'Aw, gee whiz, Mom!'"

"We glaumin' all day?" Billy asked.

Shoestring nodded.

"I'd rather do jobs for people," Billy protested. "I hate stealing and begging."

Shoestring finished tightening the strings, stood up and looked at him with a steady gaze.

"Never be too proud to beg, Rip, if you want to keep on living. I've seen kids, men, too, weak and pale and skinny, 'cause they hated to beg or steal. You gotta, now and then, if you want to stay alive out here. Remember that."

They reached the edge of town and stood a moment to gaze at the crowds already forming along the street. "Guess you and Tiny were enjoying the show last night," Shoestring continued. "Spike went easy on you both today, but don't test him again."

"Can't do nothin' to me," retorted Billy.

"Don't be too sure. He's got his ways."

They walked on, pausing now and again to enjoy the little sideshows—jugglers, violinists, ventriloquists all performing for the crowds. A pint-size lady wearing a top hat, tap-danced to the music of an accordion player. Julius Caesar stood on an upturned barrel and his deep voice resonated among the crowd. He punctuated his talk with sweeping arm gestures. People laughed and applauded in merriment at his stories, and seemed to forget the dust and drought and hard times. It was the best fun Billy had ever seen and he could have stood there all day just watching the entertainment.

"We ain't here to stand about," Shoestring said at last, gazing around and looking for targets. "We're here to work. Now, watch me." His eyes fastened on a young couple, walking arm in arm along the street.

"Missus? Sir?" He ran up to the man, cap outstretched. "Got any change for an ice cream for a starving boy?" The woman nudged her husband and he reluctantly reached into his pocket for some pennies.

"See how easy it is?" said Shoestring, walking back to Billy and jingling the coins in his cap. "Your turn."

Billy took a breath, held out his cap to a lady who was walking slowly by, and asked her for spare change. She fished in her bag and gave him a coin, scarcely looking at him.

"That's how it's done," Shoestring nodded. "Except give the ladies a smile and a wink. Tip your cap like Spike showed you. Turn on the charm. I'm working this end of the street. You work that end. I want to see lots of change in your pocket by lunchtime. Meet at the tent in an hour."

So Billy began. He found the begging became easier each time he approached someone, and the pennies trickled into his cap.

The sun shone warmly on the little town and flooded the street with bright colours. The music was full of cheer. An atmosphere of happy excitement lifted the spirits of the tired farmers and townsfolk, their cares and worries swept away for the day.

"Can you spare a penny, ma'am?" he asked a lady who stood with her back to him as she listened to the music.

She turned to him. "Billy! How nice to see you again."

Billy cursed inwardly. The very people he did not want to run into stood right in front of him. Mrs. Cooper and Katie.

Mrs. Cooper looked at him steadily. She knew he wasn't the boy he pretended to be, bold and brave and looking for adventures, but just a simple beggar.

"Still in town! Would you like to come back with us for something to eat?"

Billy shook his head, too embarrassed to meet her eyes.

"No, thank you, ma'am. Nice to see you. I better get going." He nodded at Katie and slipped away, feeling the shame of it sink into him. This way of life was all wrong. By tonight, he vowed that he'd be on his way, free of Spike's camp and Spike's methods.

"Billy!" a voice called behind him.

To his surprise, here came Katie, running to catch up. As she reached him she paused to catch her breath. "Are you leaving soon?"

"Maybe. Why?"

"Can I come with you on the train?" she asked in her whispery voice.

"You mean ... ride the rails?" He shook his head and saw the disappointment in her eyes. "Your gran would worry, and you can't travel with a skirt on or them sandals. You have to run fast and jump on real quick. And you gotta be older."

"I'm already eleven. I got other clothes to wear."

"Why do you want to leave your gran?"

"My gran is good to me, but I want to see the world, like you."

"What about your mom and dad?"

"They don't have to know. They always send me here for the summer. I just want to try it for a while."

"Well, I dunno ..." he turned away, impossible to even think of taking a girl along. "You'd have to beg, just like me. It's not your kind of life."

"I don't care. I can beg as good as you. Oh, please! Please!"

She sure was different than the girls he knew in Venn. They were happy staying in one place, but Katie seemed all caught up in running off to have adventures. Even so, a girl could never be safe on the rails. In his opinion, they had no gumption and they weren't smart or strong enough. His whole adventure would be shot to pieces just having to hang onto her so she didn't fall off the train.

He shook his head no, but she took his arm and pulled on it to turn him around to face her. "If you're leaving town, my room is right by the apple tree at the side of the house. I'll leave the light on every night." She glanced behind them at Mrs. Cooper who waited down the road. "Throw some stones up to let me know you're leaving. Or there's a ladder lying on the ground. You can climb up and knock on the window. I'll be ready any time you want."

Where did she get such notions? She knew nothing about the dangers out there. He saw the pleading in her eyes. He'd have to let her down slowly.

"Well, I'll think about it."

"I'll be waiting, Billy. Don't forget!"

She darted another glance behind her, then leaned in to kiss him on the cheek.

He stepped back, surprised. She'd seemed just a wisp of a thing, whispering and blushing, and now here she was, kissing him and begging to run off and jump a freight train. He said goodbye and walked quickly away, hoping she wouldn't follow. At the far end of the street, he paused a second to watch some jugglers toss plates in the air, and tried to take his mind off his troubles.

"Jake! I need to speak to you!" Miss Janet called to him from the side of the street. How beautiful she looked in a flowing white sundress, a dainty parasol in one hand. As she hurried to him, he caught the scent of her perfume, sweet as his mother's wild rose bush.

"Is Charles here? Where's your brother?" She looked around, searching for Tiny.

"He's back home. He's planning on coming by tonight and do his act with you in the tent."

She looked worried. "He mustn't, not tonight. Give him a message from me. Some farmers are looking for him, the police, too. They say he stole a gun, and then he stole a chicken and … and then he fired at a dog when it tried to attack him as it protected the chickens. Luckily he missed killing anyone. Is it true? I can't believe it!"

"Hell, no, Miss Janet. Tiny … uh … Charles is a good boy."

"Those men from last night went to the police! So he mustn't come back tonight. He just mustn't! They're all looking for him!"

Billy felt alarmed. He hadn't known Tiny for long, but one thing he did know. The boy did whatever he wanted and for certain he would come into town.

He put on an innocent face. "Sure, I'll tell him, Miss Janet. But don't worry. Like I said, he didn't do none of that."

"I hope not!" she said. "Be sure and warn him, now."

She turned back to the tent and Billy stood for a moment, wondering what to do. He wanted to find his friend, but he had to spend the day with Shoestring.

Tonight, he'd leave Spike's jungle and look for real, honest work as he had planned, be independent once again. Right now, his biggest worry was how to warn Tiny. But he knew, deep down that Tiny wouldn't care. Being on stage was all he cared about.

At dusk, he trudged back to camp with Shoestring after their day's work, pockets full. Spike greeted them with an outstretched palm and they handed him their coins.

"Good work, boys. You see Tiny in town? He better be back by supper."

Billy hoped the next time he saw Tiny, they'd be hopping a freight. Suppertime came and went and still no Tiny.

"I lost him," Sticky reported on his return from glauming. "We were out past Biggar and a farmer give us these sausages." He handed over a string of them. "He went behind a bush to pee, and didn't come back. I don't know where he got to."

"I got a good idea where he went," said Spike. "He's back in town. When I see him, we'll have a powwow."

Billy's stomach gave a twist. He had better get away and warn Tiny. He sat at the campfire with the others and listened to a boy play tunes on his harmonica. At last, Billy gave a big, loud yawn. "I'm turning in," he said. "I can't stay awake."

"Sleep tight," said Spike.

Billy crept to his blanket near the firepit, lay down, and waited for a chance to slip away. Night fell, and around him a few boys were in a slumber, dead to the world. Spike and some others sat up around the campfire, smoking pipes. He waited a long time for them to turn in, but the murmur of their voices went on. Billy couldn't wait any longer.

In the shadows, he quietly stuffed extra pants and a shirt inside his blanket, rolled it up and tied it with his rope, then he crept away from Spike's camp. None of the sleeping boys stirred, and no one at the campfire looked up to see him or call out. He swore to himself this was the last he'd ever see of Spike and his gang.

His feet met the rails and he broke into a run, hoping to meet Tiny returning. If he didn't find the boy in town, he planned to keep going to the Biggar railway siding and wait there till the next freight rolled through.

Tonight, the town had become one big carnival with people everywhere and the street all lit up. He pushed through the crowds, heading to the tent and heard the sounds of whistling and clapping. The show had started! He slipped around the back to look for Miss Janet and dropped his bindle in a shadowy place near the tent wall.

A burly man guarded the stage entrance and chatted with one of the actors, his back to Billy, so he took a chance and slipped past without being noticed. He stepped through the opening that led up to the stage, stood behind the edge of the curtain and peered out.

As she spoke her lines, Miss Janet tossed her beautiful coppery hair. A few children sat right on the stage at its very edge, gazing up at her, just as Tiny had last night. But Billy couldn't see him there. A little girl with black curls and large eyes caught his attention. She perched on the stage edge along with the other children, seeming glued to every word, her head tilted just so, her mouth painted red, and her cheeks powdered. He stared. She looked like someone he knew.

"Tiny! Hot Damn!! It is Tiny!" he whispered. That lunatic had dressed as a girl so he could get up close to the action.

He heard the rustle of Miss Janet's long dress and smelled her flowery perfume as she finished speaking and came toward him off the stage.

"Jake," she whispered. "You're looking for Charles? He's ..."

But a rough hand yanked Billy by the collar and dragged him backward.

"You little bum! Get outta here and don't come back!" ordered the guard. Billy shook him off and stamped hard on his booted foot, angry to be roughly treated.

"Stop that, Jimmy. Leave him alone. He's with me!" said Miss Janet.

"No kids backstage!" Jimmy glared at Billy, but backed off.

Miss Janet hustled Billy into the dressing tent. "Charles so wanted a part, tonight," she said. "But I couldn't let him go anywhere near the stage till I gave him a disguise to keep him safe."

She checked her mirror and adjusted a strand of hair, then powdered her nose, laughing softly. "Your brother! Such a character! You'd best take him home soon, but I think he's safe for a little while." She turned at the sound of applause and laughter from the tent.

"That's my cue. Wait for me after the show."

She strode out and up onto the stage, holding herself proud and tall as she became the character she was playing. Billy could almost see the transformation, as though she had some kind of magic inside that lit her up. The same magic Tiny had.

He walked along the side of the big tent and spied a small gap between the tent wall and the ground. He left his bindle outside, and crawled through the space. No one noticed except a little girl who jumped when she saw him poke his head under the canvas.

Billy watched the play from the sidelines, looking for a chance to get closer to Tiny, but the tent was packed and there was no way to reach the stage. He was amazed how Tiny made such a fine girl, even better than the real ones up there with him. He didn't think Tiny would like to know it and he would never tell him so.

As the scene ended and the curtain began to close, Tiny got in the way as it brushed past him. The sweep of the curtain caught at his wig and knocked it off his head. He grabbed for it, but too late, the moving curtain swept it along. One of the children on stage caught the wig, fumbled, and dropped it off the stage. Tiny leaned down and tried to reach for it, exposing his long pants underneath the skirt, and his boys' shoes. He jumped down to snatch the wig, then put it back on his head but the now tousled mop of hair landed at a crooked angle. The curtain had swung closed and his eyes searched for a way out. Then he made a run for it.

Clutching at his wig to keep it steady, he took a straight path down the middle of the tent. Like a rogue wind flattening a patch of wheat, he jumped over, around, and on top of people as bodies leaned to the right and left to get out of his way. An uproar of shouts and complaints sounded all the way to the back. One man caught and held him for a moment with strong hands, but not for long. Tiny kicked out, wriggled free, and kept going.

Billy didn't waste a minute. He slid back out under the canvas wall, retrieved his bindle, and hurried toward the entrance to find the boy. No sign of him there. Was he ...? No, he couldn't be! Not back with Miss Janet! Billy rushed to the dressing tent and found him sitting on the floor, still wearing the flouncy red skirt, the sparkly white blouse and the bouncy wig as he talked to her.

"Charles, we better go. You ready?"

"Wait a minute." Tiny frowned at Billy and turned back to Miss Janet. "You got another part for me in Vancouver, maybe?"

"Don't you have a home to go to?" she asked.

Tiny flashed Billy a look that said, *I'll handle this.* "Me and Jake are hobos. We don't have a mother or no home to go to. See? That bindle is all Jake's got." He gazed at her, eyes pleading. "We're hopping a train tonight, headin' west. Maybe we'll come your way?"

Miss Janet's eyes softened with kindness. "I'm going to help you, Charles. But I want to know all about you and how you came into this situation. Homeless children, so young! Where are your parents, your guardians?"

"Two minutes, Janet!" someone called.

"I don't have time, now," she said, getting up. "The play ends in half an hour and I'll go straight to the hotel. Both of you wait for me there after the show."

She searched around and found a program and a pencil, scribbled something down, then handed it to Tiny.

"Here's an address. Keep this. Just in case something goes wrong, you'll find me here next month— the Orpheum Theatre in Vancouver."

She turned to the mirror, combed her hair into place and powdered her face. "Wait for me at the hotel when I'm finished. Stay out of sight, boys, and Charles, keep the costume for now."

She took one last look at them, and left. Billy knew he'd never see her again, but thought she was one fine lady!

"We better get to the track," Tiny said. "We can't wait for Miss Janet. Spike's gonna find I'm missing and come after us."

"Why would he care?" Billy asked, feeling a sudden suspicion. Tiny sure seemed in a big hurry. "What did you do?"

No answer came. Whatever he had done, it must have been something real bad. They had better get away fast. As they hurried outside and reached the street, Billy turned to look around him, worried that the boys were out there somewhere. His blood froze. A short distance away, a tall boy with his hair greased upward, walked slowly through the crowd, head moving from left to right, searching. No time to waste!

"He's right behind us!" he hissed at Tiny, and headed into a crowd of people for cover. Tiny followed and they walked in a hurry down Main Street, trying hard not to run and bring attention to themselves.

"Tiny, why's he looking for you? What you done? We gotta get out of town," he said. "You can hang around for Miss Janet if you want, but I'm not staying."

Tiny looked down at the program he held, tucked it underneath the skirt and into his pants pocket and nodded agreement. They left the crowded streets and headed toward the edge of town, glancing behind them now and again, on the lookout for Spike.

As they passed the widow's house, Billy noticed all the windows were dark except for one upper window beside the apple tree. There, a light shone into the night. Billy saw a figure looking out. Katie. He knew she couldn't last a day on the rails. Just the sight of dirty hobos would make her flee back to her grandmother. He whispered goodbye to her as they raced along the road, then turned into a path through open fields.

—· **CHAPTER 10** ·—

SHOWDOWN

The railway track lay off somewhere to their right, but the two stayed far from it in case the gang lay in wait there. A crescent moon sat just above the fields and cast a silvery light. As they ran, only their harsh breathing and soft footfalls disturbed the quiet.

An owl hooted, and Billy figured it was the burrowing kind that live in the grasslands. Another answered the first and Tiny stopped in his tracks.

"The gang is out there. They're after us," Tiny whispered.

"Where? I don't see 'em. How do you know ..." but Tiny grabbed his arm and pinched it hard, then dragged him behind a mound of hay with surprising strength. Billy's heart pounded so hard, he was certain folk could hear it for miles.

The hooting sounded again, louder and closer. Spike's signal. He felt the hair on his arms prickle. "What'll we do?"

Tiny scrambled out of his wig, sparkly blouse and skirt and placed them against the haystack. It looked as if a lady sat there resting.

"We'll run that way." Tiny pointed away from the railway track. "Ready?" he hissed and stared around him, looking for any motion in the dark. "Let's go!"

Away they raced, stumbling over ditches, running blind. The sound of whoops and hollers echoed across the field.

"Over that way, boys!" Spike's voice! "I see 'em. Shoestring, take the other side."

Speed was all they had to get away from the gang, but Billy tripped in a gopher hole and went down. Whump! He heard running feet close by and lay where he'd fallen, frozen like a rabbit playing dead. Someone ran closer to stand right over him. He looked up and saw that it was Shoestring. "Don't move," the boy whispered. "They're after Tiny. I'll lead 'em the other way. Stay away from the track. Spike's gonna head there and wait for him to catch out. I don't know what he's done, but Spike's real mad."

"You find 'im, Shoestring?" Sticky called from somewhere in the darkness.

Billy trusted Shoestring wouldn't bring the gang over. He'd been kind to him, helped him, taught him how to glaum and beg, and taken care of his stitches. True to his word, Shoestring moved away. "There they go!" he called. "They're running back to town. Come on, gang! Let's get 'em!"

Billy heard their voices growing fainter as Shoestring led the boys away.

But Billy knew he and Tiny were still wide open for trouble.
"Tiny," he called softly. "You there?"

There came a rustling noise as Tiny stood up from his hiding place close by.

"Shoestring's leading 'em away. Spike's for sure gonna be waiting by the track in town. We'll never catch out of here. Why's Spike so mad? What you done to him?"

"If he's waiting at the track this side, we'll just go to the other side of town," said Tiny, side-stepping Billy's question. "The train'll slow down on its way in. Once we get on that freight, goodbye, Spike."

There were lots of problems with Tiny's plan. What if Spike figured out they'd do just that? What if the train didn't slow down but roared through town at high speed? What if they were still there on the tracks at sun-up like sitting ducks?

Whatever Tiny had done, Spike would not give up easily. But there was no time to worry. Tiny led the way down a rough path that wound across the fields behind Biggar. Billy could see its lights in the distance as they jogged along a fenceline. On the way, Tiny began to count under his breath. "One ... two ... three..." When he reached six, he bent to search beside a fence post among tall grasses. He tugged out something from its hiding place. "Good thing we're going this way. Didn't want to leave my bindle behind. I got Spike's money in it. We're all set."

"All his money? He's gonna kill us both!"

"Most of it. He's never gonna catch us."

The track led them around the edge of the town, and they ran through fields and past darkened farmhouses till they reached the far end of Biggar. They crept toward the track, then sat in a ditch beside the rails and waited.

"So why'd you steal from Spike?" Billy kept his voice low.

Tiny shrugged. "I just took my share. Worked hard for it and all he ever give me was nickels and dimes. I'm his star player. He won't do so good without me, and he knows it. But I can do better without him. Found his stash where he likes to hide it, in a hollow tree outside camp. Listen! Do you hear that?"

The rails began to vibrate and sing with a steady whine, and the faint rumble of a heavy freight sounded down the track. It must be loaded, thought Billy, because it chugged slower as it moved up an incline toward Biggar. The boys scrambled up to get in close, watching each car go by and looking for an open door. The wheels screeched and Billy tasted dust as he stood ready to take a leap. But all the cars were shut tight, right to the very end.

The deck was their only hope.

Tiny ran alongside the end car as it chugged by, grabbed onto a ladder and climbed, Billy at his heels. He grabbed a rung and heaved himself up just before the train picked up speed. In a few minutes or seconds even, they'd reach Biggar station where Spike waited. If they were lucky, it might travel on through. But it might just stop there and sit for hours. They needed a place to hide.

"Where can we hide?" Billy called as they ran along the catwalk. Tiny had already reached the end of this car and jumped to the next. As they moved along, he bent to pull on the bolts that fastened the hatch doors. The first five had fastenings too rusted to open.

On they went, jumping from car to car. Billy saw a red light not far ahead. The Biggar stop! Tiny tugged on another bolt and it slid open. Billy muttered a thank-you to the stars above as Tiny opened the hatch door. He jumped down into the car, and Billy followed behind. Inside, he smelled a whiff of manure, and his feet found a wooden feeding berth above the floor. They were inside an empty livestock car.

The train slowed and lumbered to a full stop, its engine rumbling. So their worst fears had come true. They were stuck here right where Spike was sure to be waiting. Billy held his breath, hoping it might move on. But the engine gave a big sigh, then all went quiet.

"Dammit. We're here for the night," Billy whispered. They crouched in the berth, listening. Bumps and bangs and swaying and jerking motions began. The railway men must be uncoupling some cars.

Above him, the hatch lid stood open, letting in the bright station lights. "Dammit, I gotta close that." Billy took off his belt and shoved one end outside the opening before lowering the lid onto it. Now the door couldn't click shut and lock them inside. From the outside it would look shut tight. They tucked themselves in and waited.

In the sudden quiet they heard men's voices. Feet crunched in the gravel along the track. The voices faded.

"Good night," someone called.

All quiet again.

They lay in the berth, snug and comfortable but the worry that they might be discovered pricked at Billy. He sat up with a jerk. Footsteps! Just one person. Coming closer. Right above them now. A pause.

The hatch opened. The dim electric lights of the railway siding washed over them.

"Hi, fellows." Spike bent down to look in.

Billy shrank back into the shadows.

"I'm disappointed with you, Tiny. You broke the Tribe rule. You stole my dough. Looks like this car is on a dead-end track. They ain't plannin' on moving it for days. Come out now, and I'll go easy on you."

No answer came, but Billy felt the warning pressure of Tiny's hand against his arm.

"We just want to get on our way," Billy answered. "Come on, Spike, let us go."

"No quarrel with you, Rip. Go if you want."

"I'm travellin' with Tiny," he said and whispered to the boy, "Just give him his dough."

"Rip, this ain't your concern," said Spike. "You're free to go."

"You ain't getting' nothin' from me," Tiny called up.

"Guess I'll have to come in there."

"You put one foot in, you'll get a bullet through it," said Tiny.

"Good one. Your gun is back at the camp where I hid it."

"Yeah? You sure? 'Cause I got it right here with the dough, and you know my aim's real good."

Spike paused, then kicked the belt inside. "You might need that to hang yourselves before you die of thirst. I'll be back in a while if you change your mind and give it up."

He slammed the hatch shut, then opened it again. "By the way, Rip, Tiny tell you his secret?" The hatch door slammed again and the sound of the bolt rasped. Footsteps faded away along the roof of the car. Billy pushed hard against the hatch door. It didn't budge.

He turned to stare at Tiny. "Do you have the gun in your bindle?"

"Nope."

"Hell! He's gone to check for the gun in camp! He'll be back soon as he finds it."

Tiny jumped down to try the door on the bottom level. Locked. Billy joined him and they searched for openings or loose planks to crawl through. The wooden slats in the walls were all fixed in place, no space wide enough for them to escape.

Billy swung back up into the berth, sick with worry. Tiny jumped upward and grabbed onto the edge, and Billy pulled him up by the wrists. He remembered Spike's last words.

"What did he mean?" he asked. "What secret?"

Tiny hesitated, then sighed. "You're gonna find out sooner or later ... I ain't no boy."

"Huh? What do you ...?"

"Real name's Charlotte. Yep, I'm a girl."

—· **CHAPTER 11** ·—
TINY

"Jumpin' jeepers! You a girl? Never would have guessed it!" Billy gaped at her and scratched his head, "... except when I saw you up there on stage ..." He stared, trying to get used to the idea of a girl strong and smart enough to ride the rails. It upset his whole take on them. All along, Tiny had been acting a part, every minute of each day and doing a good job of it, too. Sure fooled everyone.

"How'd you ...? Why did ...?"

"How'd I come to act like a boy? It's a long story."

He heard rustling movements as she settled into the berth. "I was with my family but my pa got mean." She sighed. "Weren't my real pa but he was good to me till it all changed." Her lifeless tone hinted at bleak memories. "No money coming in. Nothing to eat. This relief train come from Toronto. All it had on it was clothes stinking of moth balls from people's attics, long dresses for having tea with the queen, fancy shoes. What good was all them long dresses and fancy coats for milkin' cows? Then Mom got pregnant again and he got real mad, said if another kid on the way, get rid of one already here, an' that was me."

Billy heard her take a deep breath, and he waited uneasily for her to go on.

"Grabs me by the back of my blouse and holds me over the well, hollerin' at Mom—but she sewed that blouse real good, she knows stitching better'n anyone. So I start to pray them stitches are gonna hold, and not one of them seams tore. Not a one. Still, if he was gonna drop me, let go—I knew I was never gonna see daylight again."

Billy felt anger and disgust at such cruelty. "Mean bastard!"

Tiny shrugged. "Mom dint do nothing, too scared to say a word. So I stayed still, not moving a muscle, then he changes his mind, throws me back onto the ground real hard. Mom screams to me to git away, and I run fast to get outta there and never come back. She never come after me."

She paused a moment as if puzzling things out for herself. "I guess the new baby got to take the place of one of us. Already seven of us, mostly boys, and me the youngest. Hadda be me ..."

Her voice faded. She fumbled in her bindle, then packed some tobacco into a pipe she took from her pocket and struck a match. It flared a second as she drew on it, and Billy glimpsed her small white face, the mouth still with its residue of lipstick, her eyes staring into the gloom as her hand cupped the bowl for warmth. He felt her sadness and stayed quiet.

"Figured I better tell you, if you and me gonna be travelling together a while," she continued, her tone cheerful once again, shedding the hurt as if it had never been. "See me sneakin' off, take a piss? Just gimme some privacy, that's all. Understand?"

"Yeah. You know, I was thinking you make a better girl than a boy, seeing you in that wig and skirt," he laughed, glad to see her back to her bold and brassy self. "You're still wearing the lipstick."

She made a face and wiped it away with her sleeve.

"So, where'd you end up next? That when you joined up with Spike and his gang?"

"Nah. A farmer's wife took me in. She got set to adopt me, I guess. But I wasn't having none of it. She always wanted a little girl, and I fit the ticket. But I decide I gotta turn into a boy an' go see the world. I cut off my hair and stole a boy's clothes from a line and jumped a freight. Dint know nothing about it. Girls can't travel on freights, got no freedom like boys. Hard to pull off, pissin' and the like, but I hold it in or find a quiet place." She chuckled. "Got enough brothers to learn how to act like a boy."

"How'd you get into Spike's gang?"

Smoke rings from her pipe spiralled upward. "My first freight, I stand on this blind next to the tender, on the step, scared as hell, and hold on tight. A boy jumps on beside me so there were two of us on that step. I stayed hangin' on, hardly looking at him.

But then this mean-looking guy jumps up and tries to push in for space, but no room for three, so he shoves his bindle at me, says watch it for him, then steps over to the tender, but I couldn't hardly take care of myself, never mind that bindle!"

She leaned over to give him a draw but he waved away the proffered pipe, eager for her to go on with her story.

"The wind takes the bag and his stuff all spilt out under the wheels. He gets real mad, takes out a knife, says, 'Damn you!' and swipes at me, tryin'a cut me.

"The guy on the blind with me was Spike. He takes that man's arm and slams it against the wall so hard, the knife drops." Tiny opened her hand, fingers spread. "Gone. The guy goes white, dint say another word, bails out at the next stop."

"You the first to join Spike's gang?"

Tiny nodded. "I seen him collect all of us, one after another. Got a way about him, kinda scary, so we respect him and get good food, a place to sleep. Never hurt us. Not pervy. Kinda lonely, I guess, and likes having kids working for him."

"He sure is scary if you get on the wrong side of him," Billy said. "He always know you're a girl?"

"Never guessed till I told him," Tiny said with pride. "Told him keep it secret if he was planning on collecting boys, and he done that. I never washed in the river in plain sight, snuck around, on the quiet, like."

"I never guessed it, neither, 'cept maybe a little when I saw you on stage." Billy shook his head in wonder.

"That's cuz I'm the world's best actress. Wouldn't of met Miss Janet if my pa dint hold me over that well. Figure everything happens for a reason. I'm doing this to save my skin and when I'm settled somewhere with good people around, I'm gonna just be myself, again."

"You gonna tell Miss Janet you're a girl, next time you see her?"

"I might. Gonna be swell to see her, again. But don't you never call me Charlotte! What do they call you?"

"Billy."

"Billy what?"

Billy felt happy to share his real name with someone he trusted. "Billy Knight."

"So we gotta pass as brothers," said Tiny. "So I'm Charles Knight if any cops ask. We gotta have a story. You and me got kicked out and we got an aunt in Vancouver. That'll be Miss Janet if they want a name. I got the program with her writing on it to prove it."

"Okay. But if we get caught, you do the talking."

Sharing his real name, and knowing Tiny's story, it felt as though Billy had tied a friendship knot ... the kind that when you tug on it, that knot just grows tighter.

"What about you?" Tiny asked. "You get kicked out?"

Compared to Tiny's life, his had been a good one. But there had been a few hard moments. "No, not kicked out. But me and my blue wagon went and stood in the relief line every week, getting food thrown in it like we was all dogs, spending food vouchers and people looking at us, talking about us, feeling sorry for us. My brother and me used to line up the same way to find jobs. So I left after we lost the farm. Took a load off Mom and Dad. They moved into town to help my aunt and uncle run their rooming house. My brother already left a while before me. We did them a favour, them always scrabbling for a bite of food for us."

Tiny finished her smoke. "You hop a freight outta there?"

He nodded. "Seemed like I got some crazy clock in me, always knowin' when that whistle was gonna blow. If I went to sleep before I heard it, I always knew just when it was coming, woke up before it sounded, listened to it callin' me to get away."

"Everyone's ridin' the rails," sighed Tiny. "Is it like this all over? Why does it have to be this way, people got nothing and rich guys got millions? I see any rich guys like them Toronto folk, I'm gonna steal from 'em. Bastards!"

Billy knew different. He told her how lots of those rich folk had lost all their money in the stock market crash.

"All them bad times," he continued. "No rain, the crops kept failing and my dad couldn't pay the loan on a hundred acres he bought a few years back."

Steam hissed and they felt a rumble beneath them. The train wheels jerked, and boxcars slammed together down the line. More hisses. They were moving!

Tiny did a sitting dance in that small space, and Billy joined in, feet and arms jiggling, body bouncing. She screamed for joy, and laughed as they slapped each other on the back.

"Vancouver, here we come!" shouted Billy.

No worries, now, he thought. Except we're locked in this boxcar. He drifted into sleep, comforted by the familiar sway of the car, waking now and then to see the glow from Tiny's pipe as she lit more tobacco.

The sound of the hatch opening woke him. Bright sunlight poured into the car. Tiny lay cradled in the berth and sleeping soundly beside him. Two legs dangled down through the hatch above and Billy gaped at them, hoping not to see Spike's buckskin moccasins. But this 'bo wore work boots that had seen some wear.

"Git! No room for you," Billy called.

Tiny sprang awake and scrabbled back to the far side of the berth as the man slid down and crouched with them. He shed a whiff of sweat, his face black from smoke and cinders.

"You got room down the bottom, ain'tcha?" he said and swung down.

Another pair of legs appeared, and a second hobo slid onto the berth, glanced their way before dropping down to the floor below.

Billy stuck his head through the opening to catch some air and looked around. A few more hobos perched along the top, lazing in the warmth. The morning sun behind them caught the sparkle of dew along the deck and flecked the grey landscape with hints of gold. The freight train, a magic carpet, carried them on toward the promise of new discoveries and adventures. Billy basked in his sudden freedom. He marvelled at this puzzling and challenging country of his that beckoned him onward to enjoy its beauty. The wide blue skies smiled down at him.

They were headed west!

—· CHAPTER 12 ·—

THE MISSION

Food for the belly. Food for the soul. Free.

Billy and Tiny read the sign posted on the church door, looked at each other, and nodded. They'd go in and try their luck. To the west lay Calgary and Billy could hear the bustle and hum of the city's voice some miles distant. Beyond that, mountain peaks shimmered against the sky. He couldn't wait to explore the other side of those! Tiny had convinced him the money she'd stolen would help them both reach Vancouver and find Miss Janet. That's all she talked about—being on stage.

The two were aiming to thumb a ride into Calgary, find a store and buy some food. But Billy felt hungry now. Hungry as a damn prairie grasshopper. They had been travelling for two days and Billy had seen much that saddened him. Just yesterday, it was the sight of a woman and her small family slumped at a railroad siding. She and the two children with all their sadness seemed shaded the colour of dust. Tiny stopped to stare at the little girl resting her head on her mother's shoulder, and the baby grizzling in its mother's arms. Tiny had placed some coins in the mother's hand to help. That same day, a hobo walking up ahead of them began to stumble, his steps uneven as if he were still on a rocking freight train. He sank to the ground to lie unmoving. Billy hurried up and shook him by the shoulder, feeling his bones rattle beneath the thin flesh.

"Mister, wake up!"

At that minute, a kind station master pulled up in his car, told them the 'bo had passed out from starvation and said he'd take the man to the Salvation Army for help. Billy felt touched by this kindness but wondered if he and Tiny would ever become so hungry that they had no more strength left in their bodies.

Last night they had slept in a farmer's field and this morning had gone without breakfast. Now, drawn by the promise of a free lunch inside the church, they entered through the tall oak doors, and stood at the back to watch the minister at the pulpit. He swayed and prayed and preached to an audience of weary hobos slumped in the pews. "God, save these lost souls," he intoned. "Bring them comfort. Lift them up, heal them, bless them. Amen."

The man gazed around the church and the whites of his eyes flashed in the gloom. "Welcome, friends, and I notice two youngsters here with us today. Join us, boys."

Billy slid into a pew but Tiny walked over to a table at the side. It held some loaves of bread, a slab of butter and a coffee pot.

"Take a seat young man," encouraged the preacher.

Tiny slid in beside Billy with an impatient snort. She jabbed him with her elbow and jerked her head at the table nearby.

"Ain't much here to fill *my* belly," she remarked in a loud voice. "Why don't he ask God to put down some meat on that table and make us a sandwich!"

The preacher scowled at her. Tiny frowned back, then whispered to Billy, "Let's grab the bread and run!"

She stood to put her plan into action, but Billy pulled her back into her seat. Lightning might strike and there'd be hell to pay for stealing from a church. And even if they ran off with the food, these hobos would have something to say about it. Some twenty of them were slouched in the hard wooden pews, lured inside like mice to cheese. Billy glanced around, noting their gaunt faces. He figured they were willing to sit through this punishment and get to the reward, even if that turned out to be only bread and a cup of weak coffee.

The preacher began to read a story from the Bible about loaves and fishes, and how a loaf and a few fish had fed a whole crowd of people. Tiny shifted with impatience on the hard bench, then gave a loud sigh and stood up.

"When we gonna get our Matthew, Mark, Luke and John sandwiches?" she called out.

"Have some respect, sonny," hissed a hobo nearby.

"Come on, Billy," said Tiny. "We can do better'n this!"

She got up and marched down the aisle to the exit and Billy followed, relieved to be up and out of there.

"God bless and save you poor sinners," the preacher called after them as they escaped into the sunlight.

"God bless and save your poor sandwiches," Tiny shouted back.

Billy tugged on her arm. "Let's just go."

"I'm gonna buy some real food, try at that farm we passed on the way." She headed back along the road, leading them away from the city. "Hell, no need for us to starve, nor them, neither. A farmer always got eggs, don't he? Maybe bread, too."

"You gonna steal some eggs?"

"Well, I got all this money. Savin' some to buy a present for Miss Janet and some goggles for us."

Billy nodded agreement. He had noticed hobos wore goggles whenever they decked a train. Those sparks coming at them from the engine could be fierce. He'd once seen a 'bo with his clothes on fire from all the glowing cinders. The other fellows had rushed to help him slap them out before he went up in smoke.

"Seein' them rotten sandwiches, I feel like having a bang-up feed," Tiny went on. "Like Spike always sayin', we only got today. Could be dead tomorrow. I'd rather be fed than dead.

Don't ever want to get like that man we seen back there a ways, starvin' till he falls down. Come on, let's go find them eggs. Maybe share with the hobos a little, feed the multitude, like that preacher said."

"Just like Robin Hood," said Billy, thinking about Spike's money and how Tiny had stolen it from him.

"Who's Robin Hood?" Tiny asked as they followed the track that led away from the city.

"A man who used to steal from the rich, and give to the poor."

"Well, I ain't givin' it all away if it's gonna get us to Vancouver. But I got two dollars to spare. I could eat a bunch of eggs right now."

As they walked, Billy noticed the dry grasses and parched earth of Alberta looked no different than in Saskatchewan. Up ahead, a cluster of farm buildings lay scattered on a patch of land. They climbed over a farmer's fence and set off across ruined wheat fields. The wind moaned around them, and Billy saw the damage from dust and hoppers that this farmer had suffered, just like the damage he had seen on his dad's farm. These people must be hurting. The same raggedy clothes hung on their line, the same slime from the dead grasshoppers coated their farmhouse walls, and the dust piled in drifts along their fenceline. The breeze stirred and lifted faint clouds of it and

Billy could smell and taste its familiar stink. He couldn't wait to move on toward the ocean all clean and sparkling blue.

They found the farmer in the barn, his face weathered by dry winds and his own worries.

"Hey, mister, you got any eggs?" Tiny asked.

The man pushed his cap above his forehead to look them up and down. "Where'd you spring from?"

"Saw your farm and we got some money to pay for 'em if you got 'em."

"Sure, eggs is what I got lots of. I can give you a few."

"How many can I get for a dollar?"

"I can give you four dozen for a dollar," said the farmer. "But you don't want all that."

"I'll take four dozen. You got any bread to go with it?"

"Sure, a nickel for a loaf."

"Give me five of 'em," said Tiny. "An' butter. I need butter to cook it all."

"Joanie!" The farmer called out the barn door where a little girl was tossing a ball up in the air and catching it. "See how many loaves your ma got for these young 'uns. Fetch five if she got 'em, and a slab of butter."

"Two slabs," called Tiny. "And milk."

"What you want with all them eggs?" whispered Billy.

Tiny shrugged. "I'm hungry enough. Ain't you?"

While the girl ran into the farmhouse, they helped the man pick up eggs from a neat pile lying in an open storage cupboard, with all shades of speckled browns and whites. The farmer found a sack and placed each egg inside. "Go careful with these," said the farmer when the sack was half-full with the forty-eight eggs. "They crush easy, shells ain't as strong as they used to be when the hens got better feed. You all riding the rails?"

"That's right."

"How you plannin' to eat 'em all, anyways?"

"We got plans for 'em. They'll get et," said Billy, taking the sack and cradling it against his chest. "My brother can carry the bread and butter."

The farmer's wife walked in, wearing a neatly embroidered apron, her yellow hair tied up in a scarf. She carried a bundle wrapped in paper, and a bottle of milk. She looked curiously at them. "I only got four loaves, but there's two slabs of butter here, and the milk, too. Where you boys from?"

"Saskatchewan. Lookin' for work," said Billy.

"You want work?" said the man, eyeing Billy up and down in a measuring way. "You know how to bale hay? Milk a cow?"

"Sure do," said Billy.

"... but we gotta get going," interrupted Tiny. She glared at Billy. "Ain't got no time to stop."

"Right you are. Give 'em the food, Mary."

137

The butter came wrapped in grease-proof paper, two slabs, and Billy caught a glimpse of creamy whiteness as he took the goods. The loaves were browned on top and puffed up like clouds, and his mouth watered.

"How much I owe you?" asked Tiny.

"Eggs come to a dollar, butter twenty cents, bread forty cents, milk, twenty cents. One dollar eighty."

"Here, keep the change," said Tiny, handing him a two dollar bill.

"Best of luck fellows." The man seized the bill and looked at it carefully back and front before putting it in his pocket.

As they walked out with their feast, Tiny pointed up the road. "I seen an old pan or something along there a ways. We're gonna make a bang-up meal in that. Let's go get it."

They walked along and Billy stepped carefully so as not to jostle the eggs. After a while, he saw something blue lying in the ditch alongside. Tiny put down her bundle and hurried over there. She came back carrying a large pot lid, rusted and dented. Billy imagined it had fallen off a cart of household belongings after some family had left their farm.

Tiny placed her sack full of bread and butter and milk in the upturned lid and stepped along, whistling and humming, walking back in the direction of the church.

"You gonna feed them men?"

"We got time. Less you got an appointment somewhere?" she added.

"Guess it don't make no difference."

Back at the church, men were ambling out, ready to catch the next freight.

"Hey, fellas," Tiny called. "I got a real feast here. If you make a fire, I got the makings for a forty-eight-egg omelette."

The men looked over at Billy with his fragile bundle, and Tiny with her bread and butter sitting on the pan lid.

"What's your game, sonny?" someone called.

"What you got there, kid?" asked another, walking up to have a look. He was clean-shaven and dressed in bulky layers—two pairs of brown pants, one pair belted, the other held up by suspenders; and he wore two jackets, the inside one, grey, the outside, brown, making himself into a walking closet. As he came close, Billy saw three shirt collars under the jackets. On his feet were old and worn black boots, but he had looped a good pair of brown leather shoes around his neck, tied together by their laces.

"No game," answered Tiny. "Figure it's time for a swell lunch after them pitiful sandwiches you just ate."

The man's face brightened as Tiny explained.

"We got a ton of eggs. All we got to do is crack 'em and cook 'em."

"Well, don't that beat all!" said the hobo, turning to the others. "What do you say, fellas?"

"Reckon we can make a fire back there in that field," said a tall, skinny man with a hungry look. "Mac, go get some firewood and I got some matches."

The boys led the way to a sheltered spot and the hobos roamed around to collect twigs and whatever else they could find for kindling. "I got some Bennett blankets," said a stringy fellow with long greying hair, and he took out some newspaper that he probably used to wrap around himself on cold nights. Another fellow went off and brought back a couple of old bricks to rest under the pan, and soon they had a crackling fire.

"Show 'em, Billy," Tiny said proudly and Billy carefully laid the sack of eggs down on the ground. The hobos gathered around and peered down at them with big smiles.

"We got forty-eight of 'em," said Billy. "Fresh eggs for everyone. So start crackin'."

Tiny wiped the blue pot lid clean with her sleeve, smeared the underside with a wad of butter, laid it on the ground and began breaking eggs into it. "You seen that woman with two kids by the railroad track back a ways?" she asked. "Too bad she ain't here."

"A cop came and took her and the kids to the Sally Ann," said one of the men. "They'll look after her."

"That's good. Now you fellas can crack 'em while I beat 'em.

Got lots of good butter and milk to go with it."

"My stars, you got a feast here! Long time since I ate a fresh egg," said the clothes-closet man. "I'm a short-order cook. I'll fry up a nice omelette." He laid down the shoes and began to expertly crack the eggs with one hand and drop them, one by one, into the upturned lid.

The others piled the kindling into the makings of a good fire, gathered around the eggs and helped crack them. Tiny blended them all with her spoon as Billy poured a little of the milk into the mixture, then held the lid steady.

"Got some salt, here," said the cook, taking a paper twist out of his pocket. He shook it in. "Now we're cooking! Go easy, now. Don't spill 'em. Hold that lid steady."

There were three eggs left in the sack, and the edges of the omelette already reached the edges of the pot lid. "Lift her real careful," said Tiny as she mixed in the remaining eggs, and two men slowly and carefully lifted the lid to rest over the flames.

"Bet Miss Janet would love to see this!" Tiny said.

Billy caught the aroma of the eggs and butter. "This gonna be the biggest damn omelette I ever ate!" he crowed.

"That looks almost done," the cook said. "Lift it off and let it finish cooking away from the flame."

A couple of men used rags to lift the pot lid by its edge and laid it back on the ground till it was ready. They stood admiring it for a moment, its creamy yellow goodness, the size of it, and the fragrance that reminded Billy of a time when he was never hungry or forced to rely on the kindness of strangers.

"Okay, fellas! Time to dig in!" said Tiny. "We got enough for all of yuz so I'll dish it out. Get the bread, Billy."

The forty-eight-egg omelette went a long way among fifteen or so people. There were second helpings, and when the pan was empty, Tiny put it back on the warm embers and threw in the last slab of butter to melt it down so they could dip in the rest of the bread. Tiny and Billy drank the milk. "Good for growing boys," agreed the hobos. Bellies full at last! Billy thought his eyes must be crossed from the bliss of having a full stomach. Every bite finished, the men lazed back in the bright sunlight. Someone took out his mouth organ and played *Old MacDonald Had a Farm* and they joined in to sing along, adding ducks, hens, geese, cows, till the list was so long they honked when they should have quacked, and oinked when they should have neighed, and finally broke into laughter of the finest kind that warmed their bellies in a different kind of way.

"Well, gotta thank you two," said the cook, stretching and gathering his bindle. "Best meal I ate in a long time," said another to a chorus of agreement.

"Thank my brother. It was his idea," said Billy.

"Damn good one. Where you both headed?"

"Vancouver," said Tiny.

"You can catch out down the track that-a-way." The man pointed west. "There's a CN freight coming through that don't stop in Calgary but heads south a ways around the city."

Billy and Tiny shook hands with everyone, gathered their bindles and headed out as the group began to scatter this way and that. Billy felt happy about the morning's work.

"Miss Janet would sure be proud of you," he said to Tiny. "Wish she coulda been there to see it."

"Yeah, she's gonna adopt me mighty quick."

"You hopin' she's gonna *adopt* you?"

"For sure. Then I can learn all about acting and get some good parts."

They passed a siding with a few stranded boxcars, and found the place where the grade rose slightly and the freight would slow down. An old station beside the track stood abandoned, its doors and windows shuttered. They sat down to wait and Billy gazed toward the city and the distant mountains beyond, their white glistening peaks seeming to touch the blue sky.

"Look at them beauties," said Tiny as she stared at them.

"Never seen mountains before," Billy said. "All I ever seen is lots of space around me."

The tall buildings of Calgary, though still distant, shimmered against the prairie land like a mirage that seemed to retreat the closer they came. They would ride onward toward the province of British Columbia and he imagined how it would feel to dip his toes into the Pacific Ocean and hear the sound of its waves lapping against the shore, to enjoy all that blueness and no land to interfere, on and on all the way to China. He'd never before seen an ocean, except in pictures, and he doubted that Tiny had, either. Things would surely be good once they reached it. He leaned back on his elbows, closed his eyes, and lifted his face to the sun, felt its warmth and enjoyed the peace.

"What do we have here?" came a harsh voice. "You boys waiting for the train?" A man came stomping toward them.

"Yessir," Tiny said and smiled up at him as he stood over them. He was tall and stern looking. And he wore a uniform. A railway policeman's uniform.

"Where's your tickets? Why aren't you waiting at the Calgary station. Nothing stops here."

Tiny nudged Billy and stood up, taking off her cap to turn her blue eyes up at the stranger. Billy could see by her expression that she was inventing a good story quickly in her head.

Her eyes darkened with sadness and her voice came low. "I thought this was the station. Our mom sent us here to meet our dad off the train. He's been gone for two months looking for work and no luck. But he sent us a letter that he's coming back today! So we been waiting here, sir. Which way to the station?"

The man checked his pocket watch. "So he must be on the two-thirty express from Toronto coming into Calgary. He on the Toronto train?"

"That's the train!" said Tiny. "That train on time?"

"No it ain't," said the man abruptly, eyes cold. "There's no train comes this way from Toronto, two-thirty or any time of any day. I think you're trying to steal a ride, fellows."

"No, sir, honest ..."

"So who's your ma? Give me your address and I'll check out your story."

"She's sick in hospital and she ..."

"Shut your trap! Goddamn kids. Look at you both—dirty tramps. I guess your ma is taking real good care of you, sending you out looking like dirty hobos stealing a ride."

Billy felt his anger rise at being called dirty. He looked Tiny over and noticed for the first time her grubby clothes and face. A brown smudge of dirt decorated Tiny's forehead where she'd pushed back her hair under the cap. Her shirt and dungarees were covered with a dusty grey film—coal dust from the trains. He looked down at himself and saw the same film covering his own pants and shirt. Good thing his mother couldn't see him now. At Spike's, they'd been close to the lake and always scrubbed their clothes clean, but the two hadn't seen any more lakes since they'd left.

"Come along with me. I got a cozy place for you." The man pointed back up the tracks, one hand gesturing to them to walk ahead, the other resting on the gun in his holster. Billy threw Tiny a look as they walked. They had planned for such a situation. "If we ever get caught," Billy had said, "look like we're gonna come along peaceful, and when the bull thinks he's got us, we take him by surprise and make a run for it in different directions. You go east, I go west. That way he can't chase both of us and one gets free."

But they hadn't planned for a bull with a gun. A few hundred yards along, the three reached the siding. Four linked boxcars stood alone and abandoned on a side track, no engine, no caboose. Billy saw where this was going and didn't care much for it. He got ready to run but this man must be able to read minds. He caught him by the collar and shoved him on toward the boxcars. He looked the kind who would shoot first and ask questions later. Billy didn't want to take that chance. They reached the first car and he saw that a steel bolt fastened its door. The policeman unlocked it and pushed the door partly open.

"In you go boys. Enjoy the accommodation. You should feel right at home in there. I'll be back later to put you in jail."

Billy and Tiny hesitated.

"I said get inside!" said the guard, giving Billy another shove. The two jumped inside the hobo way—hands on the edge to heave themselves quickly up and over.

"Ha! I see you *have* done this before," said the policeman.

The two watched the door roll shut behind them with a force that shook the car. They heard the man's feet crunching away and fading to silence.

Tiny rummaged in her bindle and took out her pipe and matches. "Shit, damn!" she said. "We're in a jam now! What the hell we gonna do about this?"

— · CHAPTER 13 · —
NO GOODBYES

Billy figured that if hobos ever wrote a book of rules, it would soon be well-thumbed and grimy with smoke and cinders. The most important rule would begin at the top of Page One: "No Need for Goodbyes."

He had seen men travelling along together only to take separate paths without a backward glance or a parting word. It seemed as if they had never known one another, never once shared a crust or a laugh.

But Billy knew he would always remember Tiny.

He now stood beside her in silence, trapped in their boxcar prison as the wind moaned outside. Then with rising anger, he began to pace the boards and beat on the walls with his fists. "Let us out! Let us out!"

Tiny slumped to the floor. "Don't blow your wig. That ain't workin'. Dammit! What are they plannin' to do with us?"

She hummed tunelessly as she took out her tobacco pouch and stuffed her pipe.

Billy sank to the floor and watched her smoke rings rising toward the ceiling.

"Look! There's a hatch!" Billy pointed upward. "Come on! Get on my shoulders, Tiny. Try and shove it open."

He squatted and she stepped up, wobbled, then steadied herself as he slowly stood. She walked her hands along the ceiling as he moved along beneath, holding her ankles.

"Move to the left," she breathed. "A few more inches. Stop."

He felt her straining to push on the hatch.

"Won't budge. Locked." She jumped down and picked up her pipe again. "Wish I had my gun, I'd shoot it off."

Outside, feet crunched on the gravel and Billy moved to the door. The bolt slid and it rolled partly open.

"Step back, you!" the policeman ordered him as two hobos climbed inside. "Hope the accommodation is to your liking, gentlemen."

The newcomers gazed around as their eyes adjusted to the gloom. Each had a square jaw and cleft chin that hinted they might be brothers.

"That sonabitch!" one said as he settled into a corner. "Gonna be a night in the clink for us."

"Nah. Bastard's gonna send us to one of them prison camps, I bet," said the other and glanced at Tiny and Billy. "They catchin' kids now! How long you two been in here?"

"Too damn long," Tiny said, as she blew more smoke rings and watched them curl upward.

"This is Bennett's idea of fair play?" The first man grimaced and shook his head. "While he sits there in Ottawa, living off the fat of the land—lock us all up to die in a boxcar and them rich bastards livin' the sweet life." He hacked and spat and muttered more curses, then burst out with anger once again. "That Bennett would steal the pennies from a dead man's eyes!"

"Relief camps!" grumbled the other. "Where's the relief! Drop us in the wilderness and forget us, that's their game."

"I hope he goes to hell and damnation," his partner continued, his mind still fixed on Bennett. He took out a flask and raised it in a silent toast, "...and when he does, I'm going to get down there and make his life a worse hell. I'll fix him good."

The door slid open again, and three more drifters climbed inside, anger written on their faces.

"How long we gotta stay in here? We got our rights!"

"Have a good afternoon," replied the officer, his mouth twisted in a grin.

Billy heard more complaining voices down the track, shuffling feet, and loud protests. He had seen three cars ahead of this one and guessed they were filling up fast, as the police played their hunting game.

Their own boxcar was now half-full. Some men lay snoring,

others sat in silence, worry plain on their faces. But no matter their troubles, all sang out a greeting, a curse, or a joke as the next unlucky fellow was shoved inside by the officer. A man took out his mouth organ and idly played the first few notes of a cheerful song about breezing along with the breeze. Billy had often heard it on the radio at home. Encouraged by the tune, a man took out a comb and paper to fashion a kazoo, and one fellow tooted the song on a tin whistle. As they played and sang together in a ragged harmony, Billy thought about home the way it had been—the moonlit sleigh rides, Christmas dinner around the table, his mother's Sunday breakfasts of homemade beans and eggs and toast, the glimmer of sunlight on the little creek behind their barn, or listening to the radio with Ed. To drive away his sudden longing for what was lost, he joined in with the men to sing along.

There were some good singers among them, while others sounded like rusty gates swinging in the breeze. Tiny kept quiet and leaned forward to listen. On the second chorus her voice rose light and tuneful, and she stood and swayed to the beat, "… trailin' the rails, roamin' the seas."

The men leaned in to listen. *She's a natural*! Billy thought, proud of his friend. For the rest of the tune, the men sang each verse as she whistled along, but at the chorus, they hushed up and she sang it solo.

"You got some pipes!" they called at the finish. "You're aces! One of these days, sonny, we're gonna see you on stage! You sound just like Shirley Temple!"

"I ain't no girl!" Tiny answered, tossing her head and giving Billy a wink. "Bet I could beat her any day!"

"I didn't know you could sing," Billy said. He'd heard her whistle and hum before, but never guessed she had a voice, too.

"'Course I can sing! Actors gotta know how to sing!" she said, rolling her eyes.

The men began fidgeting and pacing. It had been over an hour since they'd entered this boxcar prison.

"How long they plannin' on keeping us in here?" complained one, taking out a pickle jar and peeing into it. "About time they let us out, ain't it?"

The glow from the sun sent a shaft of slanting light through a small hole in the door. Billy noticed the opening was positioned about where the outside bolt must be. Too small a space for his own hand, but Tiny's hand could maybe ... "Can you get your hand through there, pull on the bolt?" he asked her. "Maybe you could slide it open?"

Tiny nodded. She got up and managed to push her hand through the hole up to her wrist, feeling for the bolt on that side.

WHAM! Something heavy slammed against the door. Tiny gasped and pulled her hand back in.

"Bastard!" she yelled through the door. "You're gonna be sorry you done that, mister!"

The hobos complained loudly at this cruelty.

"He's just a kid!"

"What the hell you done that for?"

"Just giving you a taste of what you'll get for real if you try anything," came the bull's voice. "Next time I won't miss, sonny."

"You okay?" asked Billy.

Tiny examined her hand. "Just grazed a little."

"I got a clean hanky if you need to wrap it," offered a hobo. "Bastard trying that on a kid!"

"It's okay." Tiny waved away the handkerchief and gingerly placed her hand in her pocket, then grimaced and held it behind her back.

"You sure?" asked Billy, worried. "Let's see it."

"Nah, he missed. It's okay." She had turned pale and he saw sweat on her brow.

"Just lemme see it," Billy persisted, moving closer to have a look.

Tiny glared at him. "Scram!"

"Okay, okay—but how you gonna catch out ..."

He yelped as she kicked him hard in the shin. "I said belt up, dammit!"

Billy cursed, and as he rubbed his leg, the door rumbled open.

"Out you get," ordered a policeman.

The hobos stood up, stretching their stiff joints and uttering groans and complaints, then jumped down one by one. Billy and Tiny followed last. Outside, two more officers had freed the rest from the other cars, and Billy calculated there were at least thirty prisoners, their shoulders slouched in defeat as they waited for orders. The first officer told them to take a piss and all did their business beside the track, except for Tiny, who turned away. Then, in a single long line, they began to walk along a dirt road to a destination Billy could only imagine —a jail cell? A firing squad?

"Where you takin' us?" a man asked.

"You'll find out soon enough," a policeman answered, swinging his club as he marched off to the front of the line. Billy hated him with a fury, knowing by his voice and swagger that this was the fellow who had struck Tiny's hand. A second policeman walked along to oversee the middle of the line. The third followed at the end, right behind Billy and Tiny. He looked younger than the other bulls, maybe new and not as confident as he glanced ahead now and then at the policemen up front as if to follow their lead. He made his voice as gruff as theirs, but Billy guessed he felt unsure, and the stern expression he wore was all for show.

"What are you two doing ridin' the rails?" he asked, frowning.

"Kinda young, aren't you? Where's your folks?" Billy noticed a glint of interest in his eyes.

"Got nowheres else to go," Tiny answered, playing on his sympathy. "Ma can't feed us no more and she threw us out. Where they takin' us?"

"Well, I'm not sure about you two. These fellows are heading to a workcamp. You won't be much use there. They got other plans for you."

Billy didn't like the sound of that.

"Lock you in the clink tonight, and you'll go before the judge, tomorrow, I guess," the man continued. "He'll put you in a home somewhere."

"But we ain't done nothin'," Billy protested.

"Well, I guess you've been stealing rides from the Canadian National Railway," he answered in a sour tone. "That's a good enough reason. Nothing's free and now you got to pay the price."

Billy darted a wild glance at Tiny and mouthed, "*Run.*"

She nodded, ready.

The man caught the look between them and placed a hand on the club tucked into his belt. "Don't get any ideas!"

So Billy kept walking. "You got food and a place to sleep in that workcamp?" He figured he'd rather get them a place in there than a jail cell for the night.

"Nope. Kids can't dig ditches and shovel gravel."

"Please, mister," Tiny pleaded. "Let us go, it don't matter to you none. We ain't no use, ain't strong like them other fellows. Let us go and we promise we won't never ride the rails again?"

Up the dirt road stood a large horse-drawn cart. Hobos climbed up into it as the first policeman kept watch, one hand at the gun on his belt. Tiny stopped short to stare at the wagon, then turned to face the officer. She took off her cap, loosely held it with her damaged hand, and used her good hand to twist it. Billy watched as she turned the full force of her worried gaze on the policeman. *Keep at him, Tiny.*

"Letting us go won't hurt none. And we're too young for jail," she tried again.

Billy saw grazing on the fingers of her right hand, the first finger swollen and purple. The man saw it, too.

Billy held his breath. Had she worked her magic? He glanced at the guards up front. Their backs were turned. The hobos directly in front kept trudging along, too sunk in their own worries to notice.

"Okay. Scram before I change my mind," the man answered softly, jerking his head toward the railway track.

"Thank you, mister!" said Billy.

"Just get along. Stay outta sight and don't come back this way."

He turned his back on them and walked on. Tiny took the lead and ran, her injured hand against her chest, heading toward a curve in the track that branched toward the south. Billy caught up and the two pounded along together, aiming to put some distance between themselves and those officers. Now and then they glanced behind. All seemed quiet.

Billy stopped to catch his breath. "Let's wait here for that train."

"No. We gotta keep going, put more distance from them bulls!"

They began walking together at a fast clip. Tiny stayed quiet, unlike her usually chatty self. She kept her injured hand tucked inside her shirt and held against her chest. Billy didn't dare ask if he could take a look at it.

"You sure talked that guard out of throwing us in jail!" he said.

"Miss Janet's gonna love hearing *that* story," she answered as he nodded agreement. She looked him up and down in a considering way, eyes sparkling beneath the brim of her newsboy hat. "Maybe she'll give you some kinda job, too."

"That'd be swell!" Billy thrilled at the possibility. Travelling with show people in those fancy cars—what a life that would be!

Tiny began to hum a tune, and Billy hoped she was feeling better.

The setting sun spread a pale light over distant foothills and it seemed as if the mountains were creeping up the sky to put out its last rays. Tiny stopped to stare back down the track, then sank to her knees and placed her ear to the rail. As she knelt there, Billy stared again at the bruising along one hand.

"How's your ..." he began, then stopped himself, still feeling the sharp kick she had given him.

"A train's coming!" she called.

Billy crouched to touch the rail and felt it vibrate. They stood up and gazed down the track, waiting. And after a minute or two, they saw it—the freight they'd been hoping for, its smoke rising in white puffs.

"Yippee! Get ready to catch out!" shouted Billy. "I'll jump on first and help you up."

The freight moved closer and Billy saw a few hobos sitting up on deck. He began to run ahead, his feet moving fast, faster, and heard Tiny's running steps behind him. Could she keep up? Now the train moved neck and neck with him and reached a speed close to the danger zone, but Billy saw no open doorways to grab onto.

His eyes darted from the ground ahead back to the iron monster as it began to overtake them. The engineer inside waved him away and gave a warning tug on the whistle, but Billy kept on. Here came a boxcar with a ladder up the side, about ready to pass on by. He raced for it, reached up and his hand clamped tight onto a rung. He lifted himself till both feet touched the ladder, then turned to help Tiny. She was falling back slightly, feet and arms pumping for more speed, bindle bouncing on her back.

"Come on! Faster!" yelled Billy over the train's roar. "Grab my hand!"

He leaned out as far as he dared and Tiny's good hand reached up to meet his, her eyes fastened on him.

"Gotcha!" Billy gripped her and jerked her upward to stand beside him on the ladder.

But Tiny's right hand scrabbled to hold on, and he saw dried blood on her nails and felt a pang of worry. Whether from the effects of the blow or a sudden loss of balance, her injured hand slid off the rung. Billy reached out and caught her arm, held on tight, and pulled her up till they were both secure. He hugged her to him for a second, feeling overwhelmed by a sudden need to protect and keep her safe.

"I'll go first." He edged over the top and turned to see her wincing as she pulled herself up. He turned back and half-dragged, half-lifted her onto the deck, then crawled a little way along the catwalk and checked to see that she was following. At that second he saw something that caused his hopes to plummet—a black cloud slowly growing larger to fill the sky behind them, its shape shifting at the edges, rushing closer.

Tiny saw his fear and looked back, then turned to stare at him, eyes wide. He heard the familiar sound of jaws biting, chewing, devouring; saw the flash of translucent wings, each tiny body adding to the monstrous swarm of a billion hoppers that moved with relentless intent toward them till the sound of their wings became a ceaseless roar in his ears. Daylight plunged into darkness and Billy caught a last glimpse of Tiny's face, white with fear, the luminous blue eyes fixed on him, till she vanished within the cloud.

Now he could see nothing but the swarm riding on the back of the wind. He knew these hoppers. Nothing to do but shut his mouth, close his eyes and wait it out. Hard carapaces stung his face, neck and arms. Brown stinking juice splashed upward from the rails onto a deck already slippery with their slime. The train began slowing as grasshoppers, battered to death by steel wheels, lay squashed on the tracks, loosening the grip of wheels to rails. The train slid to a stop with a violent jerk and a squeal of brakes.

"Hold on, Tiny," yelled Billy, but his voice sounded muffled to his ears, and his feet lost their purchase at the train's jolting halt. He began to slip across the deck toward the edge. He braked with his toes and scrabbled to anchor himself. The roar in his ears became a cruel sound that sang out a voracious hunger. Panting with fear, eyes shut tight, he found the catwalk by touch, covered his head with his arms, crouched down and into himself and waited for it all to stop. And waited.

Almost as quickly as it had begun, the swirl and whirr of the hoppers began to ease. He felt the train jerk again, then move forward, and he dared to open his eyes. Only a few grasshoppers flew at him, leftovers from the edges of the swarm. The sky was clearing again, the dying sun casting a glow along the horizon.

"We made it!" Billy called out and wiped his face on his shirtsleeve as he felt the train slowly regain its pace. He squinted up at the sky through his fingers and saw the black cloud had receded to the south. "You okay?"

No answer.

"Tiny?"

A few hobos sat along the deck and brushed at their clothes to wipe away the brown slime. The sight of the half-empty deck sent him an answer he could not accept. He lay along the edge of the car to search below. Seeing nothing, he stood for a better view of the land around him and called her name again and again. But Tiny was gone.

—· **CHAPTER 14** ·—
NIGHT

The locomotive hurtled through the darkness. Its warning whistle struck a wailing note that echoed the pain of Billy's loss. He beat his fists against its metal side as he cried out his grief. He'd led Tiny into danger, knowing her hand was injured and she did not have his strength. How could he go on living when his choices had put an end to her life? He wanted to hurl himself into the chasm below, take the lonely death he deserved.

If only he had held her steady when the swarm hit, Tiny might now be with him; he might still be listening to her chatter as they lazed on the deck sharing a pipe and their dreams. But the machine beneath him could not feel his loss or guilt. He longed to become as uncaring as this pitiless iron monster of fire and steam that swallowed up the miles ahead.

If only ...

He walked the catwalk, passing men who lay sleeping, till he reached the tender and found a perch close to the water tank. He felt its warmth beneath the iron surface and watched the beams of the train's headlights pierce the darkness ahead and light the rails to gold. Sparks shot out below him from the friction of wheels on rails. Smoke rose up into the night and blended with his tears to sweep down his grimy face. He pulled his cap low, not caring as burning cinders danced toward him and struck his cheek and neck.

The train slowed to a stop, huffing and steaming beside a tall dark shape in the moonless night—a water tower. The hatch swung open as the fireman climbed up out of the cab and onto the roof, opened two metal lids that clanged loudly, then pulled on a rope to bring down a pipe from the tower. Water sloshed and gurgled from the pipe into one tank, then the other. As the beast drank its fill, the man glanced without interest at Billy, then job complete, slammed the lids closed, and climbed back into the cab. The hatch shut behind him and the train sped onward.

Alone again, Billy lay on the tender and without tying himself on, sank into a troubled sleep. If he rolled off the train to die in the gulf below, it was a punishment he deserved. Let this train decide his fate—take him onwards or propel him to a sudden end.

Morning light played against his closed eyes. He kept them shut tight against the day to come with all its memories of yesterday's loss. But all around him he could sense something ... a presence. He opened his eyes and sat up trembling in the chill air to a sight that made him gasp. On either side of him towered glittering mountain peaks, covered with eternal snow. He felt the strength of their stern granite faces that spoke of an ancient wisdom far removed from his own troubles. An eagle rose from its nest in a tall fir, wings spread wide as it dipped and circled above. Rushing streams chattered and beat against the rocks and poured from mountain chasms into a frothing river below. The train rallied upward through narrow canyons, over trestle bridges of dizzying height, through tunnels pitch black but for a distant circle of light that grew stronger and brighter, till it seemed to Billy he rode the back of a fiery steed that snorted and panted till it burst out into sunlight.

The cab hatch slammed open. The fireman stuck his head up through the opening. "You hungry? Come on inside, son."

Billy, shivering in his shirt and thin cotton jacket, stepped around the water tank and the man gave him space to climb down the narrow ladder into the cab. "No need to freeze your arse up there. We got some nasty tunnels coming. You headin' to the coast?"

"Vancouver."

"You got caught in the thick of 'em." The man gestured at the grasshopper stains on Billy's clothes.

Billy glanced down at his shirt and pants, smeared brown with juice. "Hate them things."

An engineer sitting at the controls gave him a nod and a grin. The fireman beckoned Billy to a nearby stool and turned away to stoke the fire. Filling his shovel from the coal hopper, he opened the firebox door and expertly tossed in a heap of coal as black dust floated around them. Billy stared in wonder at the view outside the window and the craggy mountains looming above. He imagined himself at the controls someday, an engineer, seeing the country from east to west—surely there could be no better job in the world!

The train slowed as it entered the darkness of a tunnel that led them downward.

"Kicking Horse," said the engineer, wiping a smudge of soot and sweat from his face. "Man who surveyed this site ran out of food and got kicked three times by his own horse, told everyone this was a crazy place to build a tunnel through a mountain but nobody listened and they built it anyway."

The train emerged to cross a bridge over a rushing river, then plunged through a second tunnel to trace a spiralling path that twisted back on itself like a corkscrew as it descended. Down, down, then out again, the train journeyed through a sun-swept canyon and once again racketed through yet more tunnels that offered only brief moments of darkness, or periods of time so long that Billy feared they might never see light again.

"Connaught Tunnel. Longest in Canada," the fireman explained as, through the windows, brown billowing smoke wrapped around the train. The hobos on top must be choking and Billy felt lucky to sit safely inside. An acrid stench crept into the cabin until, at last, they broke out of the smoke and into fresh air and sunlight, then travelled on for an hour before crossing another turbulent river. Its shimmering beauty caught the sun's rays, making it flash and sparkle as it tore and raged along as if racing them to an undetermined finish line.

"Columbia. All these rivers in a big hurry to get to the Pacific," the fireman explained as he picked up his shovel to pour more coal into the firebox.

"Just like me," Billy answered, and the flames leaped in agreement.

The train travelled on with a wild spirit barely contained but for the man's firm hand on the throttle, like a jockey holding tight to the reins. The men named each peak, lake and valley as if speaking warmly of old and valued friends. The engineer tended to eggs and sausage that sizzled in a fry pan on the cookstove; a loaf of bread sat on a ledge, sliced and ready; and there were three plates, one for each of them, and cups of hot coffee, while alongside, the mountains kept them company. Billy listened to idle conversation over the engine's rattle and roar and he occasionally joined in when the men threw a word or two his way, happy to sit quiet and bask in their friendship and good will. Not wishing to overstay his welcome, he thanked them at last and climbed up through the hatch. Gentle breezes touched his cheek as if the very mountains sent warm breaths to comfort him.

The sun rose higher and the train swept down the tracks as way stations flashed past, their names as rhythmic as the train's wheels—Craigellachie, Malakwa, Solsqua, Sicamous, Canoe. With his mind and spirit calmed, he let go of his sorrow and rode the train the way he had ridden his horse, Sadie, hugging its back and savouring the view that stretched ahead through the mountains, thrilling to its fierce speed, trying to forget the hard track he'd left behind as they galloped on toward a new beginning.

— · **CHAPTER 15** · —
REVENGE

Billy woke from a doze, shivering. Nighttime, and along the train's deck, men lay sleeping, or huddled together in the chill air, cigarettes glowing. Their train sat at the Kamloops station, but the kind engineer had told him that once they took on a new load, they would carry on to Vancouver.

He uncurled himself from his space on the deck, stumbled upright, and climbed down to the ground to search for shelter.

The siding was empty of railway officials. Rows of boxcars stood side by side, ready to be joined to locomotives and continue their onward journeys. Under the yellow glow of a station lamp, Billy walked the length of his train, looking for an open doorway. The end cars seemed swallowed in darkness but he found an opening in one. He paused at the doorway and heard deep breathing within. He could make out the shapes of sleeping men inside, spread about on the floor in a haven of safety. He swung up to find a space among them and lay down, his bindle for a pillow.

Their sighing breaths created a feeling of peace and he felt bonded with this company of strangers. He breathed in unison with the rest and tumbled into sleep. Some hours later, he drifted awake to mutterings and shuffling feet, but his exhaustion drove him back into a dreamless slumber until a shunting and banging awoke him. The line of boxcars was moving back and forth in steady jerks. The train must be switching lines. His eyes began sliding closed but he fought to stay awake and make sure this car wouldn't be left behind. He looked around him to find that he was entirely alone. The sleeping men were gone. Had he dreamed the presence of those others?

In the half-light outside, a hobo trudged past and Billy called out. "Is this car going on through?"

"Yep," said the man. "Stay put and get a good sleep. You'll end up in Vancouver."

Billy took him at his word. He awoke to bright daylight and utter silence. Something wasn't right. He jumped down to investigate. This boxcar was going nowhere. Now separated from the train, it sat among some others on a siding beside the roundhouse. That hobo had given him the wrong information.

He stamped his feet to get his blood moving and slapped himself up and down to beat some warmth back into his body. Surrounding mountains sloped gently toward a calm river, their sides carpeted with evergreens. A few houses stood along a dirt road and he walked across the track toward them. No one challenged his presence. He passed a butcher shop whose keeper was unlocking his door to begin the day's business. He glanced at Billy without interest. Further along, he came to a brick building with a sign that read, "Kamloops Hotel."

Hunger dug into him. There might be some work for him here in return for a meal, but if not, he'd have to swallow his pride and ask for a handout. The dust and stains on his clothes, a rip at the knee of his pants, and the broken laces on his shoes might arouse some sympathy.

"*Put your pride in your pocket,*" he could hear Mac's chiding voice in his head, and he remembered Shoestring's well-meant advice: "*I've seen people starve to death for being too proud to beg.*"

Well, he felt starved right now in a way he never had before. Without a full belly to help him think, it seemed he'd lost his entire understanding of things. *Where the hell am I going? What am I doing here? Why ever did I leave home?* He felt afraid that he might die of hunger and never reach the ocean. And what was the chance of finding any work in Vancouver? He hesitated at the closed door, then reached to open it. He would give his luck one last chance. If they turned him away here, time to give up and go home.

At that moment a truck pulled up on the road outside. He

turned to watch the burly driver walk around to slide a crate of eggs from the back and carry it toward the side of the building. He passed Billy without a glance.

On impulse, Billy called out. "Hey, mister, I'm lookin' for work. You got any for me?"

The man didn't turn or answer. Billy sat down on the step and waited. Inside the truck, a plump, dark-haired woman sat in the passenger seat. After a few minutes, the man reappeared carrying the crate, empty now, walked on by and slid it back into the truck.

"Mister, you got any jobs for me?" Billy stood and moved closer.

The woman leaned out to take a look at him. The driver turned at last. He had a mop of brown hair and a red complexion so scoured by sun and wind it might have been scraped by a wire brush.

"So you're lookin' for work."

"Yes, sir, you got any?" He would take anything, no matter what, just to see a change in his luck.

He looked Billy up and down. "Looks like you been workin' in the mines."

"I been ridin' freights. Come all the way from S'katchewan."

"So you know farming?"

"Sure. I know everything about farming."

"You ever done any hauling?"

"Yes, sir! I've hauled stumps an' all."

"What about haying?"

"Yes, sir."

"Milking?"

Billy laughed. "I can do that in my sleep."

The man scratched his head as he considered. "I can give you twenty cents a day, grub, and a place to sleep."

Billy stepped toward him. "Sounds okay to me."

"I'm an eight-hour a day farmer. Eight hours before lunch and eight hours after. You up to that?"

"Yes, sir."

The man jerked his thumb toward the back of the truck. Billy climbed in among a stack of empty milk crates, happy to have some work handed to him and some hope along with it. A few miles down the road, the truck turned off and bounced over a rough track to enter an open gateway. Billy's eyes widened as he saw what lay ahead—a sprawling ranch, with stables and riding ring, a farmhouse, and fenced meadows, everything neat and polished. Rich folk live here, he marvelled. And with green fields stretching toward the forests and mountains, he knew this land had never seen dust or drought. The truck came to a stop in front of the farmhouse, a white two-storey building with bright curtains at the windows. Billy jumped down and gazed around him, enjoying the sight of green meadows after knowing only the dust of Saskatchewan.

"I'm Todd, and my wife here is Debby," said the man. He lifted the crates from the back. Debby nodded to him in a distracted way as she went inside the house. "What's your name?"

"Billy." He figured for a real job, he would give his real name.

"Billy what?"

"Billy Knight. This is some farm! How many horses you got here?"

Todd gestured to the stables. "I manage the horses for a fellow in town. A dozen, mainly studs, but I own a couple of workhorses. The cow barn is where you'll be. Back behind the house. Sleep in the hayloft. And you'll be out in the hayfield with another boy, Métis kid, Jerry Marcel. From Saskatchewan, like you. We got some potato fields need hilling, and some clearing to do. There's a pump by the barn back there. Go wash your face and hair." He turned to go inside. "And wash up real good, use the soap. Then come into the kitchen for lunch. You can start right after."

Billy hurried to the barn. The sooner he washed up, the sooner he could get to that meal. He did as Todd ordered, scrubbing his face and neck and hair. He took off his grimy shirt, then plunged his head and shoulders into the water barrel to remove every speck of grease and dirt and soot. A ladder led up to the hayloft, and after putting on his one clean shirt and pants, he left his bindle there and hurried to the farmhouse, knocked at the kitchen door and went inside. Debby was spreading the table with plates of ham, cabbage, fried potatoes, and bread and butter. Todd sat forking in the food.

"When did you last eat?" Debby asked, as Billy gazed at the spread, eyes wide. "I'm guessing you're hungry."

"I haven't ate since yesterday," said Billy. "Sure looks good."

"Sit down." Todd nodded to him and Billy pulled up a chair, trying to contain himself and not gobble up everything in sight but show some manners. Todd paid him no attention and they ate in silence while Debby bustled in and out, seeing to one thing or another. When Billy felt he'd filled the hole in his stomach, she cut a large piece of apple pie and put it on his plate before hustling off with a basket of wet laundry.

Todd watched him make quick work of the pie and appeared to be thinking something over. "You'll get two meals a day," he said, at last. "Breakfast here and lunch out in the field. For your suppers, there's a store up the road a mile. You can buy what you want from there."

Billy didn't plan to spend his only two dollars at the store. He wished he hadn't eaten so much just now in spite of his hunger. It had scared Todd into worrying he would eat like that every day. He'd have to try and scrounge for food somewhere.

Todd told him he'd be raking hay in a field today and took him outside to point toward the meadows. "Had some rain a couple days ago but it's all dry up there now. Take that rake over there. I'm gonna fetch the horses."

Todd strode away toward the paddock where two workhorses grazed along with some sleek thoroughbreds, their coats brushed and shining. Billy took the large rake leaning against the wall and set off. He crossed to the meadows up behind the barn. There, he found a boy raking hay in long easy sweeps. He stopped his work to watch Billy's progress across the meadow.

When he reached him, Billy held out his hand. "Jerry? I'm Billy," he said.

Jerry's green eyes flashed with intelligence. He was slender and tall, his black wavy hair fastened in a ponytail. He looked at Billy's outstretched hand, hesitated a moment, then reached out to shake it.

"You from the prairies?" asked Billy.

Jerry nodded.

"So how'd you get out here? You come on the rails?"

"Mostly walked."

Jerry turned away to go on with his work. Billy took the hint and began to work alongside, raking the almost dry hay into long windrushes across the meadow. Todd appeared over the crest of the next field, sitting atop a wagon pulled by two workhorses. As the horses plodded along, blades attached to the wagon turned and raised a shower of cut grass.

The boys laboured throughout the hot afternoon. Jerry seemed reluctant to speak at all as though words were rare and precious things not to be wasted on the likes of him. Billy was sure he read contempt in the boy's eyes whenever he tried to start a conversation. After two hours of a silence broken only by the lift and swing and drag of the rakes, they saw Todd crossing the field with a pitcher of water. He told them to rest awhile.

"So you've walked real far, I guess?" Billy tried again. "You never tried hopping a freight train?" He sat down beside Jerry, enjoying the view of mountains and hills stretching around them.

Jerry chewed on a grass stem, shrugged in response, then lay back and closed his eyes. Billy gave up.

Late that afternoon, Todd called to them to go fetch some supper. Jerry turned without a word to walk away toward the woods bordering the field. Billy watched him go, then caught up with Todd as he led the horses back to the stables.

"Jerry don't talk much," he observed.

"Good worker." Todd turned to stare after Jerry. "Got a camp in the woods, guess he's set up some snares. I'll get the horses tucked in, then I got more chores for you after supper."

"Okay. I'll go wash up."

Billy walked slowly to the barn behind the house, feeling

soothed by the fragrance of fresh cut grass, and the peace of the countryside. But every now and again, the image of Tiny came to mind, and the last time he had seen her as she scrambled up the ladder to the deck. He dunked his head in the rain barrel as if he might wash away that memory, then climbed up to the loft. Below him, three milk cows mooed softly and huffled— comforting sounds that reminded Billy of the night in the boxcar when he'd lain down among strangers who had seemed to breathe as one in a kind of fellowship. He felt good to have steady work at last, and even though the pay was bad, he had no worries for the moment. He could count on two meals a day, a warm place to rest his head, and a time to pull himself out of his sadness and try to get things back on an even keel. Feeling secure, he lay on the hay-strewn boards to rest till Todd called up to him to come work again.

He fed the hens and turned the handle of the cream separator, then churned the cream into butter. When night fell, he looked for eggs that the hens sometimes left in the corner of the barn. He found one and broke it into his canteen, scooped out some cream and drank the mixture down. He would scrounge wherever he could and this was a good start.

Todd had been true to his word. The workday began at sunrise and ended long after sunset, but Billy enjoyed an easy familiarity with the routine, it came so naturally to him. After a few days, the aches and soreness in his back and shoulders from the hard labour eased a little, and the routines became second nature; up at dawn collecting hens' eggs, milking the cows, eating a good breakfast in the farm kitchen, working in the fields or hilling potatoes along with the silent Jerry. Lunch in the fields. More work. Feeding the cows and horses in the evenings, rounding up the stray chickens to shoo them into the coop, stealing a couple of eggs, drinking the rich cream, then more chores till bedtime.

He liked to watch the riders in fancy gear who drove in from town to gallop their horses over the meadows. One morning he watched a young girl in the paddock with her mother. She had come for a riding lesson and Billy could not take his eyes off her. She trotted her horse around the enclosure with perfect posture, her long blonde ponytail swinging in time with the horse's tail, together creating a picture of grace and elegance. Billy took a moment from mucking out the stable and leaned against the fence to take a rest. When she got down from her horse, he jumped over to hold the animal steady.

"You got a beautiful horse," he told her as he petted it.

She scarcely looked at him. "Take him to the stable, boy," she said. "Brush him down for me."

So that's how it is, he thought as he led the horse away. *Too good for me. I'm just a farm boy to her*. He felt very small all of a sudden, as if his idea of himself as a brave explorer had been all wrong. He remembered that even Mrs. Cooper hadn't been fooled when he had bragged to her about his adventures. He wished he had Tiny's gift for acting a part.

Todd wasn't the sort to waste time in idle chat. He spoke to Billy only as needed, reciting the list of chores each day, keeping a steely eye on Billy's work, and seeming to find no problem with his output. Billy figured he was doing a decent job. If not, he knew Todd would waste no time letting him know.

"Hens aren't laying so many eggs lately." Debby had entered the barn late one afternoon, startling him as he sat at the milk separator, churning the milk into heavy cream. "You noticed anything?"

"They seem okay to me," he answered, feeling his skin prickle with anxiety, but keeping his tone casual.

"Seems like something's stealing 'em. Maybe a fox. Let me know you see anything."

"Yes, ma'am."

She looked hard at him, knowledge suddenly plain in her eyes. "Maybe you've been eating them."

It wasn't a question. Billy knew he'd been found out.

He ducked his head, ashamed. "Yes, I ate a few. Sorry. I won't do it again."

"Why aren't you going to the store to buy your suppers?"

"I haven't got money for that."

She considered this. "I'll leave some food for you behind the well whenever I can. Don't say anything to *him*. Our secret. You ever done any baling?"

"Yes, sure. I always helped my dad on the farm."

"The migrants start work tomorrow. Todd says he'll keep you on a while longer." She turned away without another word.

So it was about time to move on, he thought. He felt ready to start his journey to the west coast. If nothing else worked out for him and no jobs to be found, at least he could say he had seen the Pacific Ocean. Instead of his usual foraging for eggs that evening, he walked across the meadow toward the area of forest where he knew Jerry had set up camp. A curl of smoke rose some distance away and he moved in that direction, curious to learn more about the boy. The sun had dipped below the horizon, spreading some golden beams of light. He saw the glow of a campfire, smelled a pungent smoke and the flavourful aroma of something cooking that made his stomach rumble with hunger. A few hundred feet away he found Jerry sitting beside the fire, his back to him, stirring something in a pot over the flames. Billy hesitated, not willing to spy on him, yet the boy had been unfriendly from the start. How would he react now to seeing him walk up to his camp? Billy stepped closer, wondering if he should call out.

"You want supper?" Jerry asked without looking around.

He had already detected his presence. Billy felt surprised to be invited by this sullen boy who hardly spoke. He walked up and looked into the pot, its contents simmering over the fire.

"Smells good!"

"Rabbit."

The boy lifted the pot from the fire with a forked branch and placed it on a flat rock, then gave him a spoon while he used his hunting knife to stab pieces of meat for himself. Billy sat down and spooned up some meat and gravy. It had a taste of wild onions, mushrooms and garlic. Behind them in the woods stood a lean-to fashioned with branches and interwoven with pieces of bark and brush.

"Tastes good. How'd you catch it?"

"Snare."

"They easy to catch?"

"Easy. Since only eight years old, I been trapping with my dad, bigger animals—fox, weasel, mink. Couldn't open the traps back then. Had to put a little stick here," Jerry motioned to show his method, "and put my knee here and put that spring down."

Billy felt encouraged that Jerry was talking to him at last. "You get good money for 'em, I bet."

He nodded. Billy slurped up the rich gravy and Jerry handed him a browned biscuit. "La gaalet. Bannock."

Billy bit into the hot biscuit, savouring its smoky flavour. "Where you headed next?"

The boy dipped his bannock into the pot. "I'm gonna stay around here, look for somethin' else when this job is finished."

The sounds of soft mooing drifted across the fields as the animals headed home to the barn. Billy finished his meal, then lay back and gazed up at the darkening sky. In the still of the evening, it felt as if he had entered a bright and safe place. *Gotta hold onto this*, he thought. *Store it away and remember good things can happen—that's what Dad would do. I ate good, got a place to sleep, someone to share the work.*

"You ride the freights here from S'katchewan?" he asked idly.

"Few times. Most of the time, I walk. Got beat up on the rails." Jerry pulled up his pant leg to reveal cuts and a long, purpling bruise that wrapped around his right calf. "Bull with a chain. They don't want Métis on their train."

Billy had learned in school about the Métis—how their leader Louis Riel had fought with the government to keep their land, but the Métis had lost it all after a long and ferocious battle against the government troops. He felt an admiration for Jerry, all alone, his people's lands stolen away by settlers. Yet here he was, still surviving with an innate skill and a strength born of need, and still open to offering his friendship.

As if guessing Billy's thoughts, Jerry built up the fire with more sticks, then lit a wooden pipe to share between them. Billy took a few puffs and gave it back. An evening hush descended and at last, Billy stood up and stretched. "Thanks for supper. I'm heading to the coast after I'm done here. You could come along, maybe?"

"I travel by myself." Jerry puffed on the pipe and stared into the fire.

"Anyway, thanks," Billy called as he walked on. "See you tomorrow."

He felt a relief that Jerry had turned him down. It was far better to travel alone. The loss of Tiny had made this clear. Life on the rails was hard enough. Best not to make any friends.

Before turning in that night, Billy checked behind the well just in case Debby had left some food there. He was pleased to find a wedge of cornbread wrapped in paper. He would save it for Jerry as payment for his supper. At dawn, the sound of a truck drawing up outside woke him, and excited voices invaded his usual peace and quiet. He looked out the little window and saw a half-dozen men talking to Todd who gestured toward a shack beyond the paddock. Billy climbed down the ladder and caught Todd on his way into the house.

"Breakfast's on the table," Todd said. "Go on in."

"Them the workers I'll be stooking with?"

"That's them."

Todd sat down at the table and held out his cup to Debby for coffee. "You can stay today, then tomorrow we won't be needing you anymore."

Billy pulled out a chair and sat, staring at Todd. "You're firin' me? Thought I was doing a good job."

"No complaints," said Todd, his manner brisk. "But I got enough help now these workers are here to start baling the fields. Work the day with them and I'll pay you what I owe you after. You can leave in the morning. I'll give you your breakfast before you go."

Billy felt as if his world had shifted. He had expected this, but imagined he might have at least a few more days' work.

"I'm heading out anyway," he said, putting a brave face on the situation. "Gotta get to the west coast."

"Hope you find some work there," said Debby and gave him a nod of encouragement. She gestured to the lunch sandwiches she was fixing for the workers and Billy knew she was signalling that she planned to leave him more food before he left.

Shy at first about joining the new arrivals, Billy walked slowly past their camp on his way to the meadow. They sat around the firepit drinking from mugs, their faces brown from working under the sun and he heard joking and light-hearted conversation. One called out to him. "Come join us, kid!"

He sat down with them and someone handed him a mug of

barley coffee and asked where he came from. "You know how to bale?"

"Sure, I know it."

He sipped his coffee as he enjoyed their jokes and the special feeling of belonging to this group, however temporary it might be.

"Let's get started," said their leader and they rose to amble up toward the meadow behind the farmhouse, where Todd had hitched the horses. Billy worked in tandem with the men, pitching the hay into the wagon for binding, setting the bales side by side in the field, listening to their chatter and jokes. He learned they always travelled together from farm to farm and that Todd was paying them fifty cents for every day. He thrilled to think he would be getting the same pay today since he was doing the same work. He looked up now and again, hoping to see Jerry, but the boy didn't appear.

At lunchtime, Billy ate sandwiches alongside them in the field, listening to their tales of life as transient workers, then he slipped away, collected Debby's cornbread from the barn and headed toward Jerry's camp. He was surprised to find him dismantling the lean-to and kicking dirt over the campfire.

"You leaving?"

Jerry slid his hunting knife into the beaded leather pouch at his belt and roped his things together.

"Finished here. Todd cheated me. Won't give me what he promised. Not working for that bastard no more."

"How much he give you?"

"Supposed to pay me twenty cents every day I work. Only paid ten."

"He promised me twenty cents, too," Billy said in dismay, "and now I'm working with those men, they're getting fifty cents. I better get the same as them."

Jerry chuckled. "Don't take nothin' for granted." He turned, ready to go. "Good luck."

"Wait a minute. Here's some cornbread that Debby made."

Jerry took the gift, paused for a moment, then raised his hand in a goodbye gesture.

Billy watched the boy turn and walk away. At the edge of the field, Jerry turned to wave, then disappeared into the shadows of the trees.

On his way back to work, Billy wondered about Jerry's life. With all the boy's knowledge of survival in the outdoors, he'd still had some bad experiences on the rails. No wonder he would rather walk than ride. And Todd had cheated Jerry. Would he also cheat Billy? It had been two weeks exactly since he started here. He did the calculations and figured that Todd owed him two dollars and eighty cents, plus extra for the stooking.

At suppertime, he approached the farmhouse. Through the

window he saw Todd and Debby at the kitchen table. He knocked on the door and Todd opened it.

"Come for my pay."

"Sure." Todd calculated the figures. "Let's see. Ten cents a day for fourteen days, that comes to a dollar forty." He turned away to collect the coins, but Billy blurted out in shock, "It's not ten cents, it's twenty cents you promised me, and I been stooking with the men all day and you're paying them fifty cents!"

"Twenty cents? You should feel damn lucky just to have food and a roof over your head. Other kids would do it *without* pay just to get a decent meal. So take the dollar forty or nothing! And I know what you've been up to with my wife! She's been feeding you on the sly."

"Todd ..." called Debby in a warning voice. She came to the doorway to protest but Todd shook his head. "She's been good enough to give you extra food." He placed the coins in Billy's hand. "And you still owe me the rest of today. You've got enough light left to haul those stumps I started on. Horses are out in the field with the wagon. Get going, then unhitch them and bring them back before dark. You can leave first thing tomorrow. Like I said before, we'll give you breakfast." He handed the coins to Billy and shut the door in his face.

Billy stormed away in fury, cursing out loud. He stomped up the ladder into the hayloft and collected his bindle. Damn it all, he would leave now, this minute. He crossed the farmyard and marched toward the road, skirting the firepit where flames danced in the half-light. As he approached the gate, he took one last look back at the farm and the view of fields and neat fencelines. A sudden thirst for revenge coursed through him, unreasoning and demanding satisfaction. Without a moment's thought, he abruptly changed course and keeping to the shadows, hurried past the barn and up the rise into the meadows beyond.

He approached the workhorses where they grazed in the back meadow, hitched them to the wagon, then climbed up, took the reins and urged them on toward the fenceline. He positioned them in front of a fence post, jumped down and fastened the tow-hooks to the post. He climbed back up onto the wagon and shook the reins.

"Haw!" he shouted. "Haw!"

The horses plodded to the left. Behind him, he heard a ripping, tearing sound. He kept going, feeling his anger burning hotter than the men's campfire. On and on he encouraged the horses.

"Take that for them mean cops and bulls," he muttered, hearing dragging sounds behind, but not looking back. "And take that for Tiny! And take that for Jerry. And that for the dumb preacher and his bread sandwiches! And take that for the poor lady and her two kids, and that, for the starving hobos, and that, and that ..."

The sounds of splintering and shattering did not stop him as he urged the horses onward. In his anger, he laid all of it on Todd. When his crazed fury had reached its limit he drooped over the reins, exhausted, and slowed the horses to a halt. He felt tired in body and soul, tired of the struggles, tired of it all. He looked behind him. The fence, twisted and tangled, spread across the field as if a giant hand had flung it down. He surveyed the damage with satisfaction. It would take a week to untangle it, repair it, and set it back in place. Served Todd right.

He got down, unhitched the horses, and fetched the feed bags from the wagon to slip around their necks. "Good old boys!" he crooned, petting them with trembling hands, his anger spent. "Good fellas!"

As he looked once more at his handiwork, he remembered Debby's kindness. His satisfaction turned to shame. Frightened at what he had done, he turned and sprinted away, grateful for the cover of darkness, and in a hurry to catch out.

CHAPTER 16

HOPE

"Where you headed?"

The speaker sat at the wheel of a blue Ford pickup. He stared out at Billy through driving rain that plashed into widening puddles at Billy's feet.

"Vancouver," he answered.

Billy had paused on a bridge that spanned a canyon so deep, he could scarcely see the bottom, only wraiths of mist rising upward as if reaching for him. A small opening in the spray revealed the rushing river far below. It heaved and tossed in waves of angry foam, its waters as black as the lowering clouds above. It offered this fleeting glimpse before the view closed up, a quick boast of its power and fury. In the noise of wind and rain, Billy hadn't heard the truck approaching.

"I'm heading south. Get in out of the wet." The man jerked his head at the seat beside him.

Billy hesitated, but lightning flashed and thunder echoed down the canyon. Shivering with cold, he took the offer. The driver leaned over to open the passenger-side door, then expertly double-clutched and revved the motor from first to third. They sped along full throttle at a whining pitch, bouncing over potholes as scatter shots of gravel hit the cracked windshield.

"I'm heading to Saddle Rock. You got any family that way?"

"Nope. Lookin' for work in the orchards." Billy noticed the man was clean-shaven, spare in build, square-jawed, his shirt and overalls spotless, his sturdy work boots polished.

"Orchards? Right now, we're in June," he said, taking a quick look at Billy, his grey eyes stern beneath strong, straight brows. Keeping one hand on the wheel, he opened a small tin and in a series of smooth motions, took out a rolled cigarette, stuck it in his mouth, closed the lid, pulled out a Zippo to light it, and puffed blue smoke.

"Won't be any orchard work till August, September," he continued. "And they get the same pickers every year. You ever picked down that way before?"

"No." Billy tensed at this information. *Should have known.*

"Likely won't be hiring if you're not a regular," the driver continued, his tone matter of fact, but at this news, Billy's hopes sank, remembering the migrant workers in Todd's fields. They travelled from farm to farm every year. He had little chance of finding work.

"Where's your folks?"

"I left 'em back in Saskatchewan."

"Farm went bust?"

Billy nodded.

"Sorry to hear it. No farmers can make a living with wheat at just twenty-five cents a bushel. You look the same age as me when I left home. I started out selling papers. Name's Arthur Evans. People call me Slim. What's your name?"

"Billy Knight," he said, giving up his real name, too tired to pick one from all the names he'd had since he left home.

"Where'd you just come from, Billy?"

"Kamloops."

Billy's legs twinged with soreness at the memory. He'd jogged along the road to put some distance between himself and Todd's farm, hoping to meet up with Jerry. He'd seen no one, but he worried Todd might be hunting him, so he'd scrambled down the bank and walked along the train track. He hopped a train but its journey was a short one, and he found himself back on the road again by dusk. As the sun dipped below the mountains, the sky became clouded and grey, signalling bad luck from then on.

Thinking back on this journey filled his mind with images of dark tracks, sleep stolen in empty boxcars, horns blaring as he stood on the road, thumb out as drivers drove on by, and a cold that made him shiver and tremble till his teeth banged together in protest.

The mountains loomed above and he wanted to reach up and shove them aside. He missed his own wide prairie lands that stretched as far as he could see.

"Where in hell is that train?" he'd muttered, thinking things couldn't get any worse. In answer, the skies had opened, and heavy rain had streamed in rivulets down his neck and back, right into his shoes. The only changes to its pattern came when gusts of a biting wind swept it horizontal and it scoured every inch of his body, trying to knock him sideways. Never had he seen such rain. If the prairies could only get some!

Desperate, he'd taken to the road again, a twisting track carved out of the steep cliffside, and he tried to find shelter in the bedraggled trees that listed and moaned in the wind. Beside him, the frenzied river swept on, cutting its path along the rock face.

Slim now questioned him some more and Billy sensed an interest and sympathy that encouraged him to open up about his travels, his parents' farm, and the troubles of drought and dust and grasshoppers.

"You been travelling all alone?" Slim asked after listening without comment.

Billy didn't want to talk about Tiny. "Not all the time," he answered. The pain of loss hurt now and again, always waiting there like an extra shadow in a dark corner.

"So I'll be turning off at Saddle Rock."

"How far is Vancouver?" Billy shivered and rubbed his arms.

"Reach behind the seat. My jacket's back there."

Billy felt behind him and gratefully pulled out a fleece-lined coat that he wrapped around his shoulders.

"You got another sixty miles to go if you want to reach the city."

Billy slumped lower at this news. During these miles, he had focused on getting through the mountains to see the ocean, find work in Vancouver, or maybe on one of the ships so he could travel on to exotic places.

Slim stared through the mud-splashed windshield, navigating a hairpin curve thrusting high above the canyon. Once this was behind them, he relaxed again. "So like I said, this time of year there won't be picking work around Vancouver or the Valley ... the Fraser Valley," he explained. "Migrant workers don't start coming up till six weeks from now. But you might find some farm work, spud or turnip picking."

"You work around here?" Billy asked, curious, thinking maybe he could give him some paid work. Slim didn't look like any common labourer, his hands clean, nails neatly trimmed.

"Yes. I work for people like you, jobless. Right now I'm visiting relief camps."

"What's that?"

"Workcamps. Slave camps. Bennett's brilliant idea. Take

young fellas off the rods, get 'em out of the cities, work 'em till they drop, pay 'em twenty cents a day. Outta sight, outta mind."

Billy had seen Slim glancing his way from time to time. Now he looked at Billy directly from top to toe before turning his eyes back to the road. "You're one of 'em. Ridin' the rails. I see cinder burns on your shirt, soot marks on your face, diesel grease on your cuffs, and you got a smell of coal-burning smoke. And yeah, you got a real hungry look, too, like you've not had a meal for ... how long since you last ate?"

"Had lunch a day back."

"So you missed a few. Way things are going, you won't get any supper." He reached behind the seat and brought out a tin lunchbox. "Some leftovers in there. Help yourself."

Billy opened the box and found half a ham sandwich. Slim gave him the thumbs up and he wolfed it down.

"So what've you been living on all this time?"

"Handouts, when I could get 'em, work from farmers." He still had a dollar in his right shoe, Todd's coins in his pocket, a hole in the sole of his left shoe, and his socks were soaked through.

"Hmm. I used to be hopeful at your age, but I only met dead ends at every turn, and took a bullet for my troubles." He shook his head. "I've been fighting for a fair deal half my life, but the problems never change. Not since I was a kid. No work. No rights. Damn stupid governments." Slim's voice faded to a mutter as if he'd forgotten Billy. Then he snapped to and focused back on him. "But you don't need to hear about all that. You'll do okay."

Billy knew he meant to be kind but it seemed his chances weren't looking good. He felt curious about that bullet he'd taken, but Slim stopped talking and bent close to peer through the pounding rain. The bumpy winding road was hedged on one side by tall firs crowding close together on craggy rock faces that rose over them, creating more gloom in this already dismal day. The windshield wipers kept up a steady beat and Billy fought drowsiness, lulled by the rhythm of the wipers and the warmth inside the cabin. He slipped into a doze till he heard the brakes grumble and the truck stopped with a lurch.

"This is where I turn off," Slim said. "You might hitch a ride from here, a few folk drive down this road to Hope now and again. Good luck to you."

Billy slipped the warm coat from his shoulders, gathered the bindle at his feet and shoved open the heavy door. The cold wind and rain hit his face.

"Thanks, mister," he called, slamming the door behind him.

Slim gave a quick wave and turned off the road onto a rough track. Billy set his bearings south along the road, all the comforts of the free ride washed away. The storm turned its indifferent face to him again, as if trying to knock him down and leave him submerged beneath this wild, tossing landscape.

He put one foot in front of the other and set off toward Hope, then heard the toot of a horn and looked behind him. Slim had backed up to the edge of the turn-off and he called something through the open window. His words were caught by the wind and lost, but Billy heard enough to know there was an offer on the table.

He hurried back up the road and Slim waved him inside again.

"I got a little job for you," he said, as Billy climbed in and they continued on down a twisting rutted track. "Nothing hard."

"What kind of job?"

"I'm making a speech to some fellows. I'll call on you to stand up and come up front. That's it. You don't have to say anything."

"You gonna pay me?"

"Ha! You're looking out for yourself. Good! Sure, I'll pay you. Twenty cents and a hot meal. That suit you?"

"Swell!" Slim's quiet manner had already put Billy at ease. Whatever the job, he felt sure he could trust this man.

Some tarpaper shacks came into view, grouped in a clearing surrounded by tall firs. In the middle stood a larger cabin where clusters of men were gathered at the open doorway sheltering from the rain. All were dressed in brown zippered jackets, grey socks pulled over the hems of grey pants, brown work boots. All looked beaten down, their faces set in hard lines, clothes dirty with the grime of mud and clay that splattered their arms and clothing. They blended as one with the backdrop of bedraggled trees and Billy felt his spirits sink at this scene of grim hopelessness.

They stared at the truck as Slim drove closer and parked.

"Hey, fellas," he called as he got out. "Billy, come along with me." He hurried with a slight limp toward the building, glancing left and right as if expecting trouble.

Billy followed, and the men made way for them, giving him curious looks. Inside, more sat at long tables, bent over cards, or magazines, or sipping from mugs. They were young, a few not much older than Billy himself. They looked up and quietened at the sight of Slim who wandered about the room, shaking hands, exchanging a laugh or a few words while the rain thrummed down on the tin roof. Then Slim walked to the front of the room and waited while everyone hushed, and all heads turned toward him, ready to listen. More men came in and sat down or leaned against the wall to watch, their gazes fixed on the speaker. Billy sat on a bench at the back, his bindle at his feet, curious to hear Slim's talk.

He began in a cheerful way. "Well, fellow workers, brothers, comrades, or maybe I should call you slaves. I've spoken to you a few times. Some of you tell me you're ready. Some are not convinced. But you've all told me the cheap cuts of beef they feed you are too tough to chew, the bread is mouldy, the milk is powdered, and the only difference between tea and coffee is the spelling. You're earning twenty cents a day to do slave labour—widening roads that don't need widening, cutting down trees that don't need cutting, shovelling dirt from one pile to another and back again."

The men laughed sourly. "You got that right!" someone called. "Twenty cents a day and nowhere to spend it!"

"What you want is real work. Work that gives you a sense of achievement. Work that pays by the hour, not the day. I know this. You know it. But all Bennett wants is to get you off the streets and out of sight."

The men hung on every word, leaned toward him, eager to hear Slim's message.

"And what kind of work is the prime minister of this great country offering? Useless work. Work that takes away your self-respect. Crummy make-work jobs. What are you earning? Twenty cents a day. You came in broke. You'll go out broke, and not only in body, but in spirit, too." Slim's voice rose to a shout. "Brothers, I'm offering you all a chance to get out of those chains!

"Thousands of us are on strike and waiting in Vancouver, ready to ride the rails to Ottawa. Men just like you. Men striking for the dignity of decent work, decent wages, and most importantly, men who want respect. If you're coming with us, then leave your slave clothing behind and get back into your rags and be ready. Start now. Make the journey to Vancouver. We've got food and shelter waiting there."

The men's voices rose in excitement, heads nodding in agreement as they discussed these promises with one another.

Slim looked over at Billy and nodded to him.

"I want you all to meet someone. Stand up, Billy. Come forward."

Billy stepped up to the front, a slight shiver running down his back from cold and nerves. A hush descended as he stood beside Slim, shoved his hands in his pockets, and faced the crowd. The men stared back, their faces expectant and curious, very much different from the defeated expressions he'd seen before. Slim had woken them up with his quiet, fierce energy.

"Found Billy on the road just now," Slim said. "Just a kid. Wheat twenty-five cents a bushel and family farm in Saskatchewan went bust. Nothing in his pockets, but lots of hope in his heart. Remember when you were Billy's age? You had dreams for a decent life, hoped to earn a decent wage. But what happened to those dreams? What's going to happen to Billy's dreams? Sad fact is, Billy's growing up to be just like you. A jobless, homeless young man."

Billy felt prickly at this description of him, but looking

around, it was easy to see what Slim meant. These men were only a few years older. Maybe they had started out just the same, but look at them now. He was already hungry and homeless. Would he end up in a slave camp, too?

"And here you all are, shoved out here in the woods," Slim continued. "The best of Canada's young men, treated worse than dogs!"

Slim's voice expressed heightened anger, and Billy felt the same anger rising inside him and he saw it on the faces of the men. Like him, they had endured hardships, but theirs had been greater. Even so, he felt like one of them, exhausted and beaten down. Had Ed been living this kind of life since leaving home? As he glanced around, he noticed one face that looked familiar, but his attention was drawn back to Slim's talk.

"They want to keep us bums all our lives!" a man shouted and others joined in with complaints of their own.

Slim nodded. "You're right, Jim! We have to put a stop to this shameful treatment, gentlemen! We do have a voice! We must use it! Join our union. Get out of those slave uniforms and back into your own rags. Leave your Bennett boots and slave camps behind! Join us in Vancouver. Get ready for a trek to Ottawa! We'll ride the rails together. Straight to Parliament! Straight to Bennett's door! Who's with me? Who's ready!"

"I'm ready," the men answered. "I'll be there!"

They stood up as one and some raised their fists in the air. "Yes! Straight to Bennett's door!"

And Billy added his voice to theirs, felt their anger as his own. "Me, too! I'm ready!" He had a lot to be angry about. Tiny, most of all. He'd do it for Tiny. He'd go with them to Ottawa.

The meeting broke up and men stood in clusters, some arguing and gesturing, others voicing their agreement with each other, all fired up with an explosive energy.

But one voice called out, "Billy! Hi, Billy! Could hardly believe it, seeing you! What in hell you doing here?"

Billy knew that voice. Images flashed of baseball games and football in bright sunshine, of swimming in the creek or listening to radio shows, of ploughing and haying, and hard work made easier by jokes and laughter. But the man it belonged to looked nothing like the boy he had known all his life. That once muscled body had become lean and bony, the face gaunt with downward lines that aged him beyond his eighteen years. And yet there was no mistaking the grey-green eyes, the red hair, and the ghost of a familiar crooked grin on his face.

That voice belonged to Ed, his one and only brother.

—· **CHAPTER 17** ·—

KNIGHT OF THE RAILS

"How's the folks?" Ed looked him up and down, his smile huge as he drew him into a hug. "You sure changed! Didn't hardly recognize you!"

Billy stared, shocked at his brother's appearance, but flooded with happiness as his words tumbled out. "You, neither! You got real skinny! I haven't seen Mom and Dad for a while. I sneaked out a month ago and been riding the rails. Lookin' for work."

Ed's forehead creased. "Dumb, stupid thing to do, Billy. No work out here. You better get on home. They must be worried sick about you."

"No, I'm not going back. Nothin' there for me. I'm going on to Vancouver with you. There's nothing back home. You know that. All them times lining up, you and Dad."

Over and over, with no money coming in, Ed and his dad had made the journey to Saskatoon to stand in a lineup and wait with hundreds of others for jobs at a factory or brewery or bakery. Their wait would end when they heard the words, "Not hiring today."

"Well, dammit!" Ed's voice rose. Billy knew Ed wasn't used to arguments from him. But he was no longer that same little brother. He'd seen a lot of the world since then, and he felt grown up now, able to stand on his own two feet. He stood without flinching as Ed's anger rained on him. "I say you gotta go home! You don't belong out here with these men, Billy. This ain't your battle. You're just a kid. You gotta get on a train headin' back east! You should be in school. No arguments. Mom and Dad need you."

"And I'm telling you, no!"

Billy's loud protest brought him the attention of several men close by. Slim stood talking with a group at the far end of the room, and even he looked over.

One man broke into their argument. "Hey, just a minute, Ed." A limp cigarette in his mouth jiggled as he spoke. "Let your brother come along with us. We need a mascot! What do you think, fellas?" He called out to the others. "Don't we all need a mascot for luck?"

"You bet, Smoky!" Men gathered around Billy and his brother, and they seconded the idea, jostling to pat him on the back or ruffle his hair. "We'll take good care of him, Ed. We need some good luck and Bennett needs to meet this kid in person. Show him what he's done, turned innocent kids into starving hobos!"

Slim broke through the crowd around Billy, and Ed called to him. "This is my brother you picked up on the road, Slim. He's got the crazy idea he's coming with us. Would you please set him straight?"

Slim looked from one to the other of them. "Your brother! Well, that's up to you, Ed. I don't want to interfere in family matters. But I must say, it's a strange coincidence you two should meet up like this. And I've always believed there are no coincidences. Whatever you decide, you should feel proud. He's a brave soul."

"BIL-LY! BIL-LY! BIL-LY!" some men chanted, and their shouts rang out as others joined in. Two men lifted Billy onto their shoulders to sit between them as they paraded him around the room. He raised his fist in anger and delight and joy all mixed together inside. His eye caught Ed's and he saw bewilderment there, fast turning into a brotherly pride that lifted his spirits even higher.

He was Billy Knight—knight of the rails! And dammit, he was ready to ride the rails with them straight to Bennett's door!

An angry voice interrupted their celebration. A thick-set man dressed in a khaki uniform stomped in followed by a group of workers, their clothes wet and muddy. Everyone fell silent, dislike for their boss plain on their faces. He reminded Billy of an angry rooster, chest puffed up with importance and glaring eyes.

"You!" He jerked his thumb at Slim, one hand on a gun in his holster. "You get out of here or I'll have you arrested and jailed. Anyone plans to strike, leave this camp! You're all blacklisted. You're not welcome here!"

"See you in Vancouver," Slim said to Billy and slipped some coins into his hand. "Your hot meal will have to wait till then." He headed for the door.

"So who's leaving?" said the boss. "Bring your relief cards to me and I'll stamp 'em. Take off those work boots and jackets. Get your own clothes and get out. You'll be arrested for vagrancy and inciting a riot when they find you back on the streets."

"We're leaving and happy to get out of this hellhole!" someone shouted and others joined in with cheers and curses as they filed out the door.

"Come on, Billy Boy," said Ed. "I'll get my stuff and we'll catch out with the fellows. Think I'll keep my boots," he muttered. "You can hide 'em in your bindle and wait for me on the road outside."

The rain had all but stopped except for a few drops from grey clouds. Billy waited as his brother ran into a bunkhouse to change out of his camp clothes. He emerged wearing ragged farm pants and his old farm boots, his strong workcamp boots concealed under his coat, looking even more thin and emaciated than before. Billy took the boots and quickly put them in his bindle, while Ed made his way inside to find the foreman and finish the business with his relief card. Billy hurried on down the long rutted track to wait by the roadside.

Men gradually drifted out as others dragged felled trees across the track to prevent vehicles from coming or going. One stooped old man carried a pack taller than himself, with odd shapes bulging through the sacking and a tobacco tin poking through the opening.

"I'm comin' with you kids," he rasped through his long white beard.

"No, Soldier," answered one. "You stay in the camp. Your arthritis plays up too much to hop trains."

The man with a cigarette dangling from his mouth approached Billy. "They call me Smoky," he said. He wore a bright yellow shirt that reflected off his yellowed skin. "You hungry?" He rooted in his sack for some food. "We have to keep Billy fed. Come on fellas, give him whatever you got! The boy looks starving."

Most came up empty-handed but a few found some apples or a hunk of bread. "Slim's gonna take care of us once we get to Vancouver," they assured Billy.

Ed stepped in beside him as the men formed a line and began to walk in fours down the road toward Hope and the next catch out. They tramped in step, spirits high as they sang marching songs. The river below roared out its presence. Like Ed, a few others had hidden their camp boots in their bindles and, when they were some distance along, stopped to put on the stolen boots. Ed began taking off his old farm boots to give to Billy.

"Looks like them shoes are shot to pieces. Toss them and put these on," he said, "and give me my camp boots. Here's some socks to go inside."

Billy felt happy to be rid of the shoes. The cardboard he had placed inside to cover a hole was now soaked from rain puddles. He put on his brother's socks, recognized his mother's knitting and felt glad of the thick wool. And with the extra warmth and bulk, Ed's old boots fit fine. He felt ready to face anything now he was back in good company. "We going to see the ocean once we get there?" he asked.

"Yes, for sure. But tell me what you been up to since you left home."

Billy told him a little about Todd and his mean nature, and then about Fingy.

"If you see that bastard again, point him out to me. I'll kill 'im," Ed said with disgust. Billy left out the story of his travels with Tiny. That memory was still raw.

"You find work anywhere?" Billy asked.

"A few jobs," Ed told him. "Went east to Toronto, nothing there. Ended up buying a bag of sugar with my last thirty cents, ate a little now and then to keep the hunger away. Went to Manitoba to plant wheat. Bunch of us. Heard the wheat gets belly-high in season. Good land that way, black soil. We were talking about how much we'd ask for pay, figured a dollar a day was fair, since the going rate used to be three dollars till wheat took a dive.

"Farmer hired us, he didn't say nothing about the rate we asked for. Just worked our asses into the ground, gave us a bed in the hay, and came payday, paid us fifty cents a day. Well, I started a union, Billy. I spoke up for the men, said to give us a dollar each for every day or we're on strike. He laughed in our faces. So I made 'em all sit down under a tree for a few hours, on strike, like."

Billy shivered and pulled his jacket tightly around him. The rain was beginning to let up and the sinking sun shed some light behind the clouds. "Did you get your money?" he asked.

"You and me know farmers hate to see men sitting idle on a sunny day," said Ed. "Time lost and maybe hailstorms or blizzards tomorrow. He came up pretty quick with our rightful pay. But I left after that and rode the rails west. Figured I'd rather die from starvation in Vancouver than die from starvation and the freezing cold back east. Should have kept at it, though. Anything's better than relief camp." Ed's shoulders slumped as he talked about camp life. "Bed bugs, rotten food." He clapped a hand on Billy's shoulder. "You and me are farm boys. We know how to work better 'n harder 'n anybody. Can't call us lazy, right? But no one sees us that way. To city folk, we're lazy bums, beggin' off the streets. You done any begging?"

"Them city folk are uppity," Billy answered, remembering the snooty girl at the stable. "Begged a coupla times. Then I got into a gang, they got into stealing. Stemming and gooseberrying they called it. So I left, came west to do some farm work, but only got ten cents a day—farmer promised me twenty—then Slim tells me them peach growers in the valley only hire the same people, so I won't have much luck pickin', neither."

"He's right. Wish I could talk you into going home. Mom and Dad moved into town, I guess? No room for you?"

"They had room, but I was thinking I'd have better luck ridin' the rails, looking for some work. Never thought we'd meet up like this."

"I sure was surprised to see you standing up there, all wet and raggedy. You look like you been through the grind. Well, I guess I'm gonna take care of you till we get to Ottawa. Maybe Slim Evans can help change our luck."

They tramped with the rest along the road while below them, the silty brown river tumbled through the canyons and Billy learned its name—the Fraser. The rain stopped and the setting sun cast its dying light. As dusk fell, he clambered up a steep bank with the others to wait beside the tracks for a catch out. Hours passed and they spent the time resting, or complaining, or snoring under their blankets.

A train approached and in the darkness, Billy saw that the

deck of every car was crowded with hundreds of men lined three or four deep. Slim had worked hard to persuade these workers to leave the camps. The engineer was in sympathy with them because he slowed the train and sounded the whistle as those on deck reached down to help pull up the others.

"Reach up. This way, kid," the men on top called. They helped pull him up the ladder. On deck, he huddled together with Ed and fell into a sleep so deep it would likely have satisfied twelve men. When he opened his eyes again, tendrils of light from the rising sun washed over a silver sea that stretched to the horizon.

"There it is," Ed said. "What do you think of it?"

It was a sight so new to Billy that he stared, silent and astonished. He had only ever known the wind on golden wheat as it rustled the tips into a flowing pathway across the fields. Now, he watched the wind set the tips of the ocean waves to shivering and foaming, an ever-changing canvas of light and stippled shade, so various and beautiful and new that he thought he could never tire of it. Behind him, the sheltering mountains created a cradle for the city that lay below.

Their train slowed to a walking pace as it reached a siding and men began to jump down and gather in a crowd, excitement plain on their faces and just one word on everyone's lips—that word spoken in groans and mutters, shouts and sighs, gasps and whispers ... "*Vancouver!*"

— · CHAPTER 18 · —
OUR BOYS!

"Hup! Two! Three! Four!"

Day three in Vancouver, and Billy marched in tight formation to the stadium, his brother beside him, the Trekkers flanking him front and behind. Sheltered by this band of men, he felt good to belong to them, alone no longer, full of purpose now and proud of it. His life had changed for the better, shifting from an unmapped and random path to a sure and straight one.

The city of Vancouver walloped him with the force of its bustling energy. Its thrum pounded in a rough and chaotic rhythm, its voice a chorus of shouts, whistles, screeches, horns, clangs, and rumbles. While the men kept their eyes front, Billy's attention was constantly drawn up, up to the tall buildings encroaching the sky. Feeling engulfed, he wondered about the people who worked up there on the top floors, imagined he must appear as a dot from their bird's eye view.

He pulled his gaze away as the army of men reached a sudden impasse straight ahead where construction workers were drilling the road. Unable to pass, the Trekkers changed their usual route to the stadium and turned to the right to march along an adjoining street, past a theatre with a flashing marquee. Billy stopped in his tracks.

"Get a move on, kid!" barked a fellow behind who bumped into him and gave a curse, but Billy hardly heard, because the sign on the marquee read *Orpheum Theatre*! Miss Janet might be doing a show there right now! A poster beside the entrance caught his eye. He slipped out of formation, checked for traffic and ducked out of line to cross the street.

"Billy! Get back here!"

He gave an impatient wave to his brother and kept moving. He pushed through a small crowd of welcoming citizens who had gathered to cheer the parade, and hurried over to gaze at the poster. One name seemed to spring out from among a half-dozen others.

Janet Walker

in

Take a Chance

And the date. Two weeks from today. Two long weeks! By then, he might be on the other side of the country, knocking on Bennett's door. But what was the use of seeing Miss Janet again? Tiny was gone. He wished she were here in Vancouver and hoped that at any second she might run up to peer at the playbill. He even glanced around searching for the yellow hair and the newsboy cap. But no point in fooling himself. He turned and hurried away to put such thoughts behind him and catch up with the men.

"Excuse me, sir, pardon me, ma'am," he said as he pushed through the line of people along the curb. A woman turned to look at him, her feet planted to stop him in his tracks.

"You a Trekker, son?" she asked, her gaze friendly and curious. Her brown hair was woven with silver grey and fastened loosely in a bun. He nodded and proudly lifted his cap in greeting, poised in mid-stride to catch up with the marchers.

"How old are you?"

"Thirteen."

"And you're riding to Ottawa with our boys?"

"Yes, ma'am."

"Well, would you like to come over for a good dinner tonight? I've been helping the boys with hot meals and baths. It's the least I can do."

Billy felt drawn to her motherly interest. It made him think of home.

"Sure. Can I bring my brother?"

"Yes! Bring your brother. What's your name?"

"Billy."

"Here, Billy, I'm Evvie. Let me write my address for you."

She scribbled directions in a little notebook, tore out the page and handed it to him. "It's not far. You turn right at the corner here and keep going four blocks. We're in a two-storey walk-up. I'll set you both up for a good meal. Five o'clock."

Billy took the folded paper with thanks and hurried to get back in formation.

He would be glad to have a home-cooked meal and so would Ed. The last three days on the streets had been full and exhausting. Last night, Billy and Ed and a hundred others had slept on beds of straw inside a hall with only one toilet and one wash basin. Each morning the men marched to the stadium to pick up two daily meal vouchers for entrance to city cafés and diners.

Slim Evans began each day with a talk and kept up their spirits with his plans for their trek. "Work and Wages! That's what we're asking. Fifty cents an hour for honest labour, the right to workmen's compensation, the right to form a union, get rid of the soldier bosses and the slave camps! Fight the good fight, Gentlemen! Stay calm and orderly. Be polite! No panhandling! Keep clean! No thieving! No drinking!"

Billy stood with Ed on street corners, handing out paper tags in exchange for donations, each tag with a string attached and a message—*When do we eat? Forward to Victory!* He felt happy to stand with his brother and the men in his unit, pursuing together this dream of honest labour for decent wages.

"Help the camp strikers! ... On to Ottawa," he chanted with the rest as he rattled his can and heard the satisfying clink of coins dropping in. He felt proud that now he was not begging for himself, but helping the cause.

After that day's work, Billy and Ed made their way to the small apartment building where Evvie lived. As they walked up to the second floor, a door opened above and Evvie peered over the railing to greet them with a welcoming smile. Ed introduced himself.

"Come meet my husband Bert," she said, wiping her floury hands on her apron before shaking hands.

In the living room, her husband looked up from his newspaper.

"Make yourselves at home, lads," he invited, gesturing to some comfortable chairs in front of the electric fireplace. "Only two of them tonight, Evvie?"

"Yesterday, we had four for supper," she explained. "We're all doing our part, giving you boys some mothering and a good meal." She turned to her husband. "They're so young, Bert! Too young to be away from home. It breaks a mother's heart. I'll go put supper on. I'll call you when it's ready." She paused on her way to the kitchen. "Bert, show them where the bathtub is. I bet they haven't had a real bath, with hot water, for ages. Right, boys?"

"Thank you, ma'am. I can't think of a better thing than a hot bath," Ed agreed.

Billy and Ed took turns in the bathroom down the hall, and washed themselves from head to toe with scented soap. Feeling refreshed, they sat down to a full meal and listened to Bert gently teasing his wife.

"Every day, my Evvie brings home some young man or other. Tell 'em about Mother's Day last month, Ev," said Bert. "Stanley Park," he went on, "those mothers formed a heart shape around the men, hundreds of boys inside that heart ..."

"Those brave boys," his wife broke in. "We think of you all as our boys, so young and so hungry and no decent work anywhere and the government turning a blind eye. And those miserable workcamps! I wouldn't put a dog in those camps! They should be stopped. We made sure the government people sat up and took notice that day, but I guess the mayor will only be happy when you're all out of his city."

They lingered for a while in the warmth of Evvie's kindness, sharing stories of their travel on the rails. The evening was too soon over and they reluctantly said their goodbyes at the door.

"Hold on, boys," Evvie called from the doorway. "Take this address. I got a niece in Regina—Kitty, short for Katherine. My brother's kid. She works at his place, the La Salle Café. Look her up. Tell her I sent you."

Ed took the paper with Kitty's address and they hurried back to the stadium, late for another meeting and more talks.

Billy knew some were tiring of all the marching and speeches and impatient to move onward.

Smoky, their unit leader, kept an eye on Billy and took care to make sure he never went hungry. "Getting enough to eat, son?" he asked each day. Ever cheerful, he easily kept up the morale of his men. But one morning he surprised everyone when he began complaining about Slim Evans. He waved the page of a newspaper he'd been reading.

"He's a Commie, you know. Says right here. Wants us to join the Communist Party so keep your eye on him and don't let him indoctrinate you all. We're a democracy so watch out for him and them other Commie bastards."

"Slim is sticking his neck out for us, and that's something no one else is doing," Ed protested. "One whole year I've been looking for work, and some of you for much longer, and until now, not one Canadian has lifted a finger to help us. Not till Slim Evans joined us. Now people are on our side. All because of him. Slim is okay by me, whatever you want to call him."

Billy stared at his brother, happy to see a spark in him at last, and a new purpose. The year on the road had changed him, and not only in the gaunt face and thin body. He had always been the funny one, the trickster, laughing and playing jokes. At the workcamp, Billy had felt shocked by the look of hopelessness in his eyes. But that empty look was fading away little by little since he and Ed had joined Slim's army.

"When are we leaving?" the Trekkers asked each other. They were surviving on just two meals a day. Each night, Billy stayed up late with his brother, wandering the streets of Vancouver so they could sleep late and avoid the hunger pangs of missing breakfast.

Another day of speeches and marches made Billy feel as impatient as all the rest. He explored the streets with Ed, always heading first toward the ocean where they stared out at its glistening waves, never tiring of its beauty. But good news came at last. The mayor arranged for a CPR train with extra cars added to take them all east, bound for Ottawa.

Their evening of departure turned cold and wet. Billy and Ed collected their bindles and marched in their divisions along the streets toward the track. Crowds of citizens lined the roadside to cheer them on. Billy picked out Evvie among them, waving a Union Jack.

At the siding sat the longest freight train he had ever seen. He and his brother lined up with the others and walked smartly alongside as hundreds of men ahead swung up onto car roofs. Billy climbed up with Ed and sat on the crowded deck to watch the Trekkers fill the deck of the next car and the next. When only half their number had boarded, not a square inch of space remained, yet there were still hundreds more waiting below. Those others would board another train tomorrow.

The train rumbled to a slow start as cheering crowds ran alongside, waving and wishing them a safe journey. He had never felt so proud in his life to be a part of this band of men.

"Remember this moment," said Ed. "Don't ever forget it. We're all going to make a difference, get our lives back. And it starts here!"

The sway of the box cars lulled Billy like a rocking cradle, and the wheels played a special rhythm that beat into his very bones. He stood to gaze around him at the changing landscape. He had begun this journey alone, as carefree as a light prairie breeze. Now bent on a common goal, he enjoyed a fellowship he had never before known. He felt the men's single pulse of determination, as if all their hearts beat as one, and he viewed the lined, tired, worried faces of those around him as one face— the face of the Trekker. In each man's eyes he saw the same spark of hope that he too felt, a hope that would drive this army forward to the next town, the next city and right on to Ottawa and up to Bennett's door.

This trek would surely make a difference, and change their lives forever.

—· **CHAPTER 19** ·—

HOLD THE FORT!

The café was dimly lit. Ed opened the door and began to walk in, but a girl stood in his way as she reached to turn the OPEN sign front to back.

"Sorry, we're closed," she said, tightening her mouth into a thin line that did nothing to hide the laughter in her eyes. She looked from Ed to Billy with impish curiosity.

"You must be Kitty." Ed stepped back onto the street as she took out her keys to lock the door.

"Only my friends call me Kitty," she retorted. "And I've never met you in my life."

"I'm Ed. Your Aunt Evvie sent us to say hello. Said to expect a real friendly girl who'd give us some coffee and pie."

She paused a moment in the open doorway, the beginnings of a smile lit her face, then disappeared. She shook her head and her brown eyes gazed at them. Billy could still see the hint of a grin on her face. "Big fat lie," she said. "And where'd you meet my aunt? I bet she never said to give you coffee and pie. You do look skinny as a rake, though. Bet you got on her good side and she took pity on you. You're with those Trekkers, I guess, riding the rails. Now you expect me to feel sorry for you. Well my Aunt Evelyn has a heart of gold, but not me, it's my day off and we're closing early. In case you didn't know, it's July the first, Dominion Day."

"Aw, come on Miss—since I'm not allowed to call you Kitty— you don't look like one of them people who don't care a damn. Look at my poor little brother here. If you can't feel sorry for me, at least feel sorry for Billy. I mean look at him and see if it don't break your heart to see his tired body crying out for some good nourishing food."

Kitty turned her brown eyes to Billy and winked at him. He looked from one to the other, puzzled. They were talking as if they'd always known each other. He'd never seen Ed act this way with a stranger. She stepped out and shut the door behind her.

"Well, I guess you'll have to come along to my place since you're so lost and homeless," she said, as she locked up. "My auntie wrote me a few days ago to tell me all about you two coming to Regina, and so I guess I gotta take care of you awhile."

"Ha! I knew you were teasing. Nice-looking girl like you couldn't be so mean."

"Nice-looking, am I? That the best you can do?"

"For now," said Ed.

Kitty shook her head at Ed as if there were no hope for him and turned her gaze back to Billy. "Bet your brother's got better manners. What's your name again?"

"Billy."

"Come along, Billy," she laughed, grabbing his hand and tugging him down the street. "You and me are going to be fine friends, I can tell."

Billy let himself be pulled along but turned to glance back at Ed who ambled along behind wearing a big grin, as if he'd been hit over the head and was trying to get the stars out of his eyes. Kitty chatted with Billy and never gave Ed a moment's notice. She led them into a grand house explaining that it had been chopped up into small apartments. Up the stairs they climbed to a little flat under the eaves that she shared with a nurse who was working a shift at the city hospital.

"Have a seat, boys. Billy, do you want some milk with your supper? I got meatloaf. And Ed," she turned at last to his brother, "I got a beer to go with it. I'm gonna turn on the baseball game while I fix it. Our own team is playing the All-Stars right here at the stadium."

"That would be swell, Miss," Ed replied as he sank into an armchair and gazed around the flat. "I knew there was a game going on in town. We were planning to watch it down at the stadium before the meeting. I haven't seen a game or listened to a radio since I left home, but I put you first. I owed it to your Aunt Evvie to look you up, like she told me."

"Such a sweet talker! Well, I guess you can call me Kitty, since your brother is so good and nice and makes up for you," she called as she prepared a meal in the little kitchen. "Will you boys go back home now? I hear Bennett stopped the Trek. And then Arthur Evans went on to Ottawa to talk to him but lost his temper."

When Billy had first heard the news that Slim failed to convince the Prime Minister to help the Trekkers, it had hit hard. "We come all this way," he had complained to Ed, "and now Bennett won't let us go to Ottawa?" He had been excited to think that he might meet the Prime Minister in person. But worse news had come. *Bennett Rejects All Demands*, screamed newspaper headlines. Bennett had ordered them back to the workcamps and blocked them from going further.

"You heard right," Ed was saying. "Slim got nowhere with Bennett. The Mounties are blocking us, but we're not giving up, we're meeting tonight down at Market Square. Eight o'clock. Slim will find a way out of this. Says we'll walk to Ottawa if we have to. He won't quit. He got us this far."

As Billy sat at the kitchen table to eat, he thought about their rough and tumble journey here from Vancouver. Slim had arranged rest stops along the route, and town folk had greeted them with warming campfires and hot food. A barber had trimmed Billy's hair along with the rest of the men. Such welcomes had helped the Trekkers riding on deck to endure the poisoned air of smoke-filled tunnels, or the bitter squalls of winds and weather.

Each station and whistle stop had evoked memories for Billy of the people he had met along the way, scenes unwinding in his head like a film spool in reverse. And when the towering mountains of British Columbia gave way to the rolling foothills of Alberta, he had remembered most of all a forty-eight-egg omelet and a runaway girl who had left him with a scar that never would heal.

By the time they reached Regina, a city surrounded by the familiar rolling plains of the prairies, folk were lining the streets to welcome them. And not as hobos, but heroes. Newspaper reporters followed their progress. "Our Boys Trek to Ottawa," screamed the headlines. Billy wished his mom and dad could have seen him, a Trekker, marching along the streets with these brave men and sparked by their goal to make a better life.

Now, Billy finished his meal and began to feel drowsy. He sat in an armchair with a cushion behind his head and closed his eyes, only half-listening as Kitty and Ed talked and joked like old friends. He woke up from his drowse when he heard his name spoken.

"They want to send us away," Ed was saying, "get us processed at another camp. I don't trust them. Billy is going back home to Mom and Dad. Me, I'm sticking with Slim."

Billy sat up. "I'm not going home!" he protested. "There's nothing for me back there ... I'm going on with you."

Ed shook his head at Billy and turned away to talk with Kitty.

Billy leaned back again and remembered the note he had left on the kitchen table. *I'll be back when I got a hundred dollars and a car.* He still had only the dollar he'd started out with and some loose change left from the money Todd had paid him. He'd spent the dollar he had earned for chopping wood— no chance of making ninety-nine dollars more ... and a car? How little he had known then. And how foolish he would look to his mom and dad, coming home with nothing.

This journey had its share of hard times, but new adventures glimmered at every turn of the track. He was restless to move on again, to keep exploring and discovering the surprises that might be waiting just around the next corner. Like his dad said, even in tough times there would always be some wonder in store. Maybe he would cross the ocean on a steamer ship to the lands beyond. There was no end to the places he might go. Whenever a train whistle echoed from a railway line, it seemed to speak just to him. "Catch a ride beneath the stars. Lots more to see. Come on!"

"You trust Evans don't you?" Kitty was asking Ed.

"Yes. I trust Slim Evans more than anyone I know, except for my brother here," Ed replied, the familiar light of loyalty in his eyes. "And you are going home, Billy."

"No! I'm gonna keep going, riding the rails with you."

"This isn't your battle, Billy. You're too young."

"What a shame," Kitty broke in to prevent an argument from brewing, "that Bennett won't help you at all."

"Thanks to him, it's no work, no jobs, no income, no marriages, no families, no future." Ed spat out these words, his brow creased in anger.

"Things will change," soothed Kitty. "Things have to change. We're all rooting for you boys. You're our heroes. Let's listen to the game a while, take our minds off our problems."

Billy liked the way their problems had become hers as well, and by Ed's open look of admiration, so did his brother.

"It's almost eight," said Kitty at last. "I'll come to the Square with you. I'd like to hear Arthur Evans."

"Swell, come along. He's asking for donations tonight but he's a good speaker," said Ed, nudging Billy fully awake and getting up. "You won't be disappointed."

On their way Ed joked with Kitty, a bounce to his step as cheerful as the Dominion Day bunting that decorated the streets. She turned to wait for Billy to catch up, then tucked his arm into hers so they were all in step together. Market Square was a large plaza surrounded by shops and hotels. A few hundred men were already gathered around a loosely constructed stage in the centre, and crowds of interested city bystanders looked on, all quietly waiting for Slim to appear.

Billy pushed forward with Ed and Kitty. As they waited, a furniture van drove in from their right and parked at the edge of the Square. They noticed another van parking to their left.

Ed looked around toward the back.

"Another one behind us," he muttered. "This doesn't look right."

The crowd hushed as Slim and his men stepped up to the stage. The same fierce energy burned in Slim's eyes and when he began to speak, his resonant voice sounded strong and determined.

"Friends, comrades, sisters, brothers ..." he began.

A commotion from below made him pause. Blue-uniformed city police were pushing roughly through the crowd. They closed in and stepped up to surround Slim and his men. Slim tried to flee the stage but an officer blocked him, then handcuffed him.

"Hold the fort, men!" Slim urged, raising his fists to show bound wrists.

As officers shoved him off the platform, his words were lost to shouts of protests from the Trekkers, then to rising cries and screams from bystanders somewhere behind. Billy heard a shrill whistle, looked around and saw city police in blue uniforms and helmets emerging from a police garage. They gripped baseball bats, holding them upright from waist to shoulder, and pushed with relentless force across the Square.

Billy's attention was riveted to these men and he could taste terror at the back of his throat. He felt the force of the panicked crowd pushing and shoving to get away. But the van doors swung wide to block them and Mounties burst out from their hiding places. They wore breeches with a yellow stripe down each side, guns in their holsters, and steel helmets that shone in the dying sunlight. They lined up in single file, gripping leather batons and riding crops, reminding Billy of a child's tin soldiers in a make-believe battle.

But there was nothing make-believe here. Ed froze in place and gripped Billy's arm, his eyes searching for an escape, but they were blocked in every direction. A whistle blew loud and long and the officers sprang to life. Thick as clouds of angry hornets, they swarmed into the seething crowd, baseball bats swinging wild onto the heads and shoulders of Trekkers and innocent bystanders. The sickening thud and crack of their weapons blended with cries of pain from the victims.

In the confusion, Kitty grasped his hand, Ed reached for Kitty's, then linked together the three pushed against the current and found their way into another stream of people escaping toward the streets behind the parked vans.

"This way!" Ed herded them through the throng and they pressed past opposing surges of police and Trekkers. In the confusion of rushing crowds, screams and cries, Billy heard the sudden clatter of horses' hooves somewhere ahead. He looked up to see Mounted Police moving swiftly forward to raise their clubs and swing downward at the Trekkers, driving them back till Billy, helpless and crying out with fear, found himself swept along against his will. He fought to stay on his feet or be trampled to the ground. Nearby, a baby carriage tipped over, the baby lying there for a second in its blankets before the child was scooped up by its sobbing mother just in time to avoid a horse's hooves.

"Billy, get Kitty home." Ed pointed to the street beyond. "That way."

Then he let go of Kitty's arm and turned away.

"Ed! Where you going?" called Billy, moving toward his brother.

Kitty gripped his arm and pulled him close. "Stay with me."

"No. Let go, Kitty."

Billy tried to shake off her hand, but her strong hold never faltered as she half-dragged him away with her. He caught one last glimpse of his brother stooping to pick up something from the street, then striding into the advancing thrust of police and Mounties. Billy could hardly bear the flood of love and fear he felt for Ed as he lost sight of him among the shoving, panicked crowd.

CHAPTER 20

PAYBACK

A white cloud rolled toward Billy as a canister hit the ground.

"Tear gas! Those bastards! Get away! Cover your eyes!" Kitty let go of his arm to clutch her face. The stinging gas had already found its way into Billy's eyes and throat. Pain was all he knew and his mouth burned as if he had swallowed fire. He felt himself knocked about by rushing people. "Kitty?" he gasped, but no answer came.

He moved away from the poisoned air as quickly as his stumbling steps allowed and drew in one precious breath after the next until the painful spasms lessened. He could dimly see again through a stream of tears.

He had reached a broad avenue outside Market Square. No sign of Kitty. To his left, hundreds of Trekkers were forming a line and he moved closer, intending to join his friends and find Ed. A hand grasped his arm and pulled him close. "Get beside me, Billy," said a man he knew from his unit.

Billy stepped into the line. He could see a horse troop of

Mounties assembling up ahead. Then a stillness hung over them, unexpected and ominous. Only the whinnies of horses and the clatter of hooves on pavement broke the silence.

"Stand firm!" came a shout from somewhere in front, whether Trekker or Mountie, Billy couldn't tell.

At that moment, with grim and silent intent the Mounties surged forward.

"Pull back! Pull back!" the Trekkers shouted.

"Back to the stadium!"

"In formation!"

The men stumbled into ragged lines of four.

"Hold the fort, for we are coming ..." they sang, faintly at first. Their voices gathered strength and the words of the battle song rang out loud and clear. *"Union men be strong..."*

Billy pushed into a row and stepped in time, adding his voice to theirs as they marched toward the stadium. He sang loud and moved briskly along, arms swinging in time as he had been taught. But as they rounded a corner, more Mounties loomed from the shadows and burst galloping out of side streets to ride among them. Billy heard the sickening thud of clubs striking down, left and right. A Trekker marching beside Billy crumpled to the ground. Blood gushed from a head wound. Billy looked up to see a horse and rider towering over him. He threw up his arms to protect his head and stood frozen like a frightened prairie grouse, heart pounding as the officer's club raised high to strike. But a flying rock hit the horse on its neck and the creature veered away before its rider could finish the blow. Billy backed off as horse and Mountie crashed into a lamppost. The officer sat in the saddle, stunned, and more Trekkers surged forward, cursing and throwing rocks. The horse swung around. Its front hooves struck out in terror as it half-rose on its hind legs, then cantered away.

"Leave them alone, you bastards!" yelled some brave citizens who watched from the sidelines. They booed and harangued the police and shouted support for the Trekkers. Billy bolted away from the struggle to find a safer street or an empty alley. He heard the sound of smashing glass as a storefront window beside him shattered. His nerves jolted and shook as if some unwieldy engine sputtered inside him. At the curb, a police officer was beating a man to his knees. The club smashed down without mercy. Billy turned his face away, helpless and unable to watch.

Nearby a cluster of Trekkers began to push parked cars into a line across the avenue. Was Ed among them? A cannister clattered at his feet. He darted away as a cloud of poisonous gas rose, then made for a nearby laneway, running as fast as his legs could carry him.

A short distance from the battleground, he heard the purring of bicycle wheels. A boy pedalled toward him, legs moving like pistons, basket filled with rocks. His clothes were neat and clean and he looked too young to be out here alone.

The cyclist steered crookedly, his feet pumping hard and Billy ran to catch up. What was he planning? The rider reached the now lengthening car barricade and emptied a basket of ammunition—rocks, bricks, and pieces of concrete, onto the growing mound. Trekkers piled up the rocks and broken shards as more children ran to add to the pile. When the cyclist turned back, Billy called out to him.

"Want some help? Wait for me!"

The boy scarcely paid him attention, only gestured to Billy to come along. Down laneways and around buildings he cycled, with Billy fast behind. He lost sight of him, glimpsed him turn a corner and caught up again at a construction site. Here, in the fading light of evening, the space seemed filled with small scurrying shadows—boys and girls gathering as much ammunition as their arms could carry, running back toward the battle site a few streets beyond. As Billy watched, two older boys lifted up slabs of concrete and smashed them heavily onto the pavement to break into pieces.

The cyclist reloaded his basket and Billy helped as his new partner nodded in silent approval. Together they held the bike steady, now too heavy to ride.

"We gotta push it," panted the boy. He wiped dust and

sweat from his face and Billy glimpsed eyes that shone with excitement. They each took a handlebar and running as fast as their load allowed, guided the bike between them toward the battle site. On the way, a wounded Trekker loomed out of the shadows, startling them as he limped past, blood dripping from his ear and cuts on his face. Billy helped dump the bricks near the defence line, a barrier of cars that the Trekkers had pushed into the middle of the avenue.

"You coming? Hurry up ..." called the boy as he cycled away for another load.

Billy began to follow but stopped for a moment to look back at the scene. Trekkers were calmly assembling in two long rows behind the completed car barricade. Each man held an armload of rocks. Across the line, Mounties and city police were lining up in formation, guns in their belts and clubs at the ready. Billy realized that with no guns or horses, the Trekkers had little chance of winning this battle, but even so, they stood strong. He knew they would take whatever came and give it back twice as hard. They might be knocked down to lie bleeding in the street, and their dreams along with them. But one thing was certain. They had right on their side. They would fight for meaningful work and fair pay and they showed it now with heads held high, bodies tensed and ready.

As Billy watched, a Trekker called out, "Payback time!"

"They started this, we're gonna finish it!" shouted another. "Stand fast, boys!"

In that moment, the Mounties charged and thundered toward them.

"Now! Give it back to 'em!" called a Trekker.

As one, the men hurled rocks to rain on the heads of the police, then ducked down to offer a clear path for the second row to aim their missiles overhead.

Billy knew this was his fight, too. He belonged here with this army, not back with the children and watching from the sidelines. He remembered Slim's words. "What's going to happen to Billy's dreams? Sad fact is, Billy's growing up to be just like you—jobless, homeless ..." He was only a boy now, but when he reached their age, would he still be drifting like tumbleweed across the country? He must give everything he had at this moment to help them win, no matter the cost. He ran to the pile and filled his pockets with stones, then with another load in his arms he stepped into the back line and stood ready.

—

Slim had always commanded his men to show restraint and courtesy, but in the thick of battle, Billy knew there was no room for kindness. The Mounted Police were easy targets as they towered on horseback above them. He could feel the explosive anger and disappointment of each Trekker spreading like a contagion and he caught their fever, proud to stand shoulder to shoulder with the best of them, and feeling the power of each man down the line. Their anger fuelled his own.

The men hurled their missiles at the oncoming Mounties. In turn, Billy gripped a rock, felt its size and heft, pulled his arm back as if throwing a baseball, but stopped in mid-throw, suddenly unwilling to hurt another human being or strike someone's husband, or father, or son. At that moment, a cannister landed nearby and poisonous white smoke rose toward him.

He could help in a different way! He dropped his armload of rocks, shielded his face and held his breath, then bent to pick up the cannister before it could do its damage to eyes and lungs. He tossed it back, smoking, over the barricade. Other cans landed on the Trekkers' side and Billy ran to as many as he could and flung them back.

"Throw 'em over! Give it back to 'em," the men shouted and others stooped to pick up the cans rolling toward them.

Their assault of rocks and returned tear gas was working! The police began to fall back.

"We got 'em!" shouted the Trekkers. "Get to the stadium! Form up! Double march!"

Billy stepped into place among the lines of four. "Left, right, left, right," came the command, and with jogging steps they moved away, voices ringing in victory. *"To battle or to die ..."*

The avenues were dark and streetlights cast flickering shadows. As he double-marched through the streets, Billy smelled smoke and the bitter odour of sweat and blood. Only a few more blocks to go until they reached the stadium and safety. There, they might regroup and count their numbers, plan their strategy and bolster their spirits. And he might find Ed.

But the sound of galloping hooves made them falter and glance behind with rising terror. A mounted troop exploded from the shadows and pounded toward them. Riders with clubs in hand were poised to strike them down yet again. Billy heard the crash of broken glass and saw a horseman drive a man through a plate glass window. Billy ran for his life, fleeing down an alley to the back of a darkened furniture store where he found shelter behind a row of rubbish bins. He crouched there, trying to calm the loud beating of his heart, and quell the anger and fear that sparked so fiercely it must surely be visible. More men followed to shelter there in the shadows. A Mountie on horseback paused at the alley's entrance, and unable to see them, he rode on.

"Let's get 'im," muttered a man beside him and he rushed to the street, took aim and pitched a rock at the policeman. To

Billy's horror there came a flash and the sharp crack of a gun. The man dropped.

"He got me," he moaned and clutched his knee.

Men ran out to help him. "Shame! Shame on you!" they yelled at the retreating rider. "Let us be, you bastards!"

But their friend lay unable to get up. "I can't move my leg. Help me, fellows."

"He needs a doc."

"He took a bullet. Get him to the hospital!"

"Somebody get an ambulance. Take him to the café, boys, we'll send help there."

Men gently carried him away and Billy watched them go, his teeth chattering, body trembling with exhaustion. He must find Ed. The night was thick with the sounds of skirmishes still raging along streets nearby. Was his brother somewhere out there, hurt and alone? Was Kitty safe? He turned onto an avenue where a few men lay dazed and wounded. An ambulance waited. Attendants were lifting the injured onto stretchers and Billy peered at each face, searching for a glimpse of red hair, hardly believing the dark and dangerous world around him. But he'd let his guard down. Behind him came the sound of a policeman's boots on pavement.

"You! Stop where you are."

The hair on his neck prickled and he dodged away, but too

late. A hand jerked him back by the collar, then gripped his arm.

"Empty your pockets," ordered the policeman.

His heart pounding, Billy turned out his pockets, full of the stones he'd never used.

"Ha! You're one of 'em. You're coming with me. We've got a cell for you, boy."

The sound of cuffs jangled and Billy began to wriggle and squirm to loosen the man's hold. "Let go, you bastard! Let go!"

From a neighbouring street a bullhorn blasted a command.

"SPREAD OUT, MEN. FIRE AT WILL."

A volley of shots echoed through the streets. A car crawled by, something flashed and a bullet pinged against the wall of a building beside them. The policeman's grip loosened. Billy seized that moment to shake his arm free and get away. As he ran, gulping sobs rose from his chest and he stammered, "... damn them ... didn't want no fight ... peaceful like Slim said, and look what they done ...!"

With the stadium blocked he had only one place left to go. He didn't stop until he found the street he was searching for. Kitty's street.

—· **CHAPTER 21** ·—

BLOCKED

Kitty opened her door to Billy's knock. "Billy! I was so worried." She pulled him inside and looked behind him, searching. "Ed not with you?"

"He's not here?" Billy stepped inside. He trembled from head to toe and his teeth clattered together like jangling coins in a pocket. He leaned against the wall for support. "A Mountie tried to catch me but I got away." He took a shuddering breath. "I hope they didn't get Ed. They were shooting at us! A Trekker got hit. In the knee. He couldn't walk anymore. What if they got Ed?"

"But *you're* okay? Not hurt? I grabbed a hand when they threw that tear gas at us." Kitty guided him into the kitchen. "Thought it was you but found it was some other kid. Where did you get to?"

"With the Trekkers, helping them fight," Billy answered sinking into a chair. "We gave it to 'em, for sure."

"You're exhausted. Well, thank God you're okay. We'll go look for Ed as soon as it's safe. Go wash up and I'll make up a bed for

241

you on the Chesterfield and bring you a hot drink and a nightshirt."

When Billy was settled in his makeshift bed, Kitty brought him some hot cocoa to soothe him. He tried to sleep but images of the night's terrors crept into his dreams—clubs poised to strike, menacing shadows, sounds of thundering hoof beats. Several times in the night, he sprang awake from violent dreams of being hunted down and he listened for Ed's step on the stairs or his voice at the door. In the early hours, the door to the flat opened and he sat up with relief.

"Ed?"

"Who's that?" came a woman's voice. A light came on. "Kitty? You here?"

"It's okay, Marie." Kitty appeared from her bedroom, yawning. "This is Billy, one of the Trekkers. He's staying here till we find his big brother. Maybe you saw him at the hospital—Ed Knight?"

"We had a lot of wounded come through," said Marie, unpinning her nurse's cap. "I'm exhausted. Hardly had a bed for every one of them. I didn't pay attention to names, just too busy bandaging and helping the docs." She looked at Billy who sat up wiping sleep from his eyes.

"You're kinda young for all this. You caught up in it, too? The streets are a mess out there. I had someone walk me home, no streetcars running."

For the rest of the night, Billy fought to stay awake and

listen for Ed, but drifted off into a light sleep till daylight. That morning, he stepped outside with Kitty and they made their way under a grey sky through avenues strewn with debris—shards of glass, broken bottles, smashed concrete. The La Salle Café had remained untouched, but they passed many shops with windows broken. Groups of city police guarded the streets around the Square, standing in clusters, glancing at them as Kitty and Billy hurried past. The smell of tear gas still lingered, echoes of the night's terrors.

They found Ed at last in a ward at the hospital, groggy, his head bandaged and a brace on his shoulder.

"Ed, what did they do to you?" Billy gazed at his brother, happy to see him alive. "They try to kill you?"

"Hi, Billy. You okay?" Ed slurred his words and looked at him through half-closed eyes.

"Whatever happened?" Kitty asked, worried.

Ed grinned, then winced. His free hand touched the bandage on his head.

"I'm glad you're safe, Billy." His eyes met Kitty's. "And is that my girl?"

"Your girl? Billy call the doctor," laughed Kitty. "That damage to his head is worse than it looks."

Ed tried to raise himself to a sitting position but flopped back on the pillow with a groan.

"Well, are you someone else's girl? Bring him to me—I'll give him what for."

"Just tell us what happened."

"Don't know ... don't remember much ... fighting ... noise. Think I picked up a piece of wood and knocked a helmet off a policeman's head, then got a blow to my own head. Heard a crack. Collar bone. Woke up in a cell. Slim in the next cell, raised a hell of a fuss—'Get him a doctor!' Doc checked me over—here I am." He gazed at Kitty. "Remember you, though."

His eyes began to close, but they snapped open again to rest on Billy. "Go on home. It's over. Just go home, Billy. Venn. Kitty, make him."

"No," Billy said. "I'm gonna keep going with you."

Ed gave a bitter chuckle. "Not jumping any freights with my arm in a sling. Anyway, I'm staying to raise money for Slim's fine. Get him out of jail...."

Ed's eyes closed and they left him to sleep.

"You'll stay with me a while till Ed's better," Kitty said in a comforting way as they walked back. They stepped over a pile of glass on the pavement and noticed a blue baby blanket lying forgotten in the gutter. In Market Square, the furniture vans were gone and clusters of people stared unbelieving at smashed storefronts and spoke together in anxious tones. Along the streets around the Square, workmen hammered boards over gaping windows and crews shovelled up debris into waiting trucks, putting the city back together again.

"The Trek is over, Billy." Kitty stopped to gaze at the destruction around them. "Just like Ed said. You'll stay a while and then he wants you back home. I think he's right. Evans is in jail. The Trekkers are giving up. We'll listen to the news on the radio, later."

"Okay," sighed Billy, "but I'm going down to the stadium to see what's happened to my friends."

She placed a warning hand on his arm. "Don't. The police will be all over that place. You'd best stay away. I can't make you, but you don't want to be picked up for vagrancy. They'd send you back to the workcamps."

"They won't get me."

Billy promised to meet her at the end of her workday. He took her advice and kept his distance from the stadium but walked along a nearby street to get a glimpse of how things looked. Barbed wire blocked the entrance and blue-uniformed city police stood guard. He found the railway station filled with Trekkers and Mounties, all milling about but with some sense of order—men were climbing into trucks parked outside, more were lining up on the platform to board a waiting train. Their faces showed defeat. Railway officials sat at a table, issuing tickets to a long line of men, and writing down names in a thick notebook.

Billy picked out Smoky waiting to board, ticket in hand, and hurried up to him.

"Smoky, where's everyone going?" he asked, worried to see the men breaking up.

"We're finished," he answered, face full of gloom, spent cigarette stub bobbing between his lips. "I'm heading back west—back to the workcamps. Bennett's blocked us." He gestured to the trucks. "Those men are heading to the Dundurn camp near Saskatoon. But I got my ticket to ride the cushions back west in style and two meals a day. What about you? Where's your brother?"

"In hospital but he'll be out soon."

"I wouldn't stick around, if I was you. A cop got killed. God knows how many Trekkers wounded, maybe dead. We're not welcome here." He pulled a half-smoked cigarette from his shirt pocket and struck a match on his shoe, spat the finished one from his mouth and quickly inserted the next. "Slim Evans! Didn't I already say? Should never have listened to him! Where did that get us? Nowhere! But it's an election year. And people won't forget us, what we did here. We'll vote Bennett out. Things have to change." He gestured to the lineup for tickets. "You're not far from home, son. Get a ticket and go see your mom and dad."

He shook Billy's hand, then ruffled his hair for good luck.

The long line inched forward and he watched Smoky board

the train with the rest. The men leaned out the windows and a loud chant rose among them in a steady cry of defiance.

"Are we defeated? Never!"

Billy waved goodbye, moved by their refusal to be beaten. He had grown to love these men. Their courage would stay with him, always. As the train pulled away and out of sight, their chanting voices grew fainter before fading to silence.

Billy hung around the station most of that day, watching more Trekkers drifting away like straw in the wind. He felt like an untethered horse—no commands to obey but missing his herd. Their mission had guided and filled his every waking moment but now that life was over. But the same eagerness to keep roaming still burned inside him. He might take his free ticket home as Ed wanted, but he planned to stay only a short time with his mom and dad. There was nothing for him there. The farm life he loved was gone.

"Hi, Billy!" called a familiar voice from across the platform. Ed stood there grinning and waving with his good arm, his right arm in a sling and a Band-Aid on his forehead.

Billy hurried over. "You're out! How's your arm?" He gazed up at his brother, noting the sparkle was back in his eyes.

"Good arm's fine. They wanted to free up my bed so they let me out. I expected you'd be home by now, Billy. Why are you still here?"

"Waiting for you to get better! You ready to move on?"

"You mean ride a freight?" Ed gave a sour laugh. "Not with a broken collarbone. I'm staying on here. A bunch of us are raising money to get Slim out of jail."

"I can help," said Billy, excited with the idea. "I'm good at collecting money—all them times I stood on the street ..."

But Ed's expression turned hard and Billy's words faltered.

"You're going home. No argument, Billy. I've got a room here with some other fellows. No place for you to stay. You've had your adventure. Go get a ticket and get on home. I'll come visit sometime soon."

"No! I want to keep going. And I can help you and Slim, too!"

But Ed gently pulled him toward the ticket line. "If I have to drag you into that train, I'll do it," he said. "Bad arm or not, I'm still bigger and stronger than you."

So Billy joined the line and under Ed's watchful eye, asked the station master for a single ticket north to Venn. He spent his last night on Kitty's couch. Ed came along early the following morning to walk him to the station.

"I'll come see you so stay put at home till I get there," Ed said, hugging him roughly with his good arm. "Don't start wandering again. Promise me."

"I'll go home but I'm not promising I'll stay," he answered. He couldn't explain it to Ed, but he felt he was just like his cat

Blackie—a wild thing not meant to live within four walls when there was a whole world waiting to explore just outside the door.

Billy boarded the train north, "riding the cushions" in comfort though he knew the view was better up on deck. From the window, he gazed at the same blue sky with not a cloud in sight, and at the never-ending dust that covered fencelines and robbed the landscape of colour and life. The boarded-up farms and dry cracked earth reminded him the hard times were not over. Nothing had changed. Nothing except for him. He felt different, older and stronger and eager for new vistas. He thrilled to the idea of riding the rails again, eastward bound, the urge to keep moving roiling within.

The sight of Venn's grain elevator towering in the near distance brought him a mix of excitement and anxiety about what lay ahead. He hoped his mom and dad would be more happy he had returned, than angry he had left. It felt good to be going home for some peace after the turmoil of the last few days, and he could hardly wait to enjoy his mom's cooking again. For a few days at least, he could count on three square a day.

As his train pulled into Venn station, he remembered the thrill and embarrassment of his first catchout—Mac yanking him back from certain death beneath the train wheels and the mockery that followed. He stopped beside a ditch alongside the dirt road and helped himself to some caked earth that he crumbled in his hand and rubbed over his face. He set his cap firmly over his hair to cover up its tell-tale colour. He hurried up Main Street, past the village grocery where men sat chatting to pass the time of day. The grocer, Mr. Carlson, who had always saved him *Zane Grey* adventure stories from his store library, watched him go by without a sign of recognition. Good. His plan of mischief might work.

He knocked at the door of the rooming house where his parents now lived and, as he waited, caught his reflection in the window. He saw a hobo with a dirty face and ragged clothes.

His aunt Mary opened the door, a bucket and mop in hand.

A memory of Tiny's face performing one of her dramatic scenes, a glistening tear poised to run down her cheek, gave him inspiration. He bowed his head in a humble manner and wrung his hands.

"Please, Miss," he quavered. "I'm starving hungry and ain't et for a week. Do you got something to spare, maybe?"

She looked him over, the light of sympathy in her eyes. "I'll bring you a sandwich. Wait there."

She began to close the door firmly in his face but he stuck his foot in.

"Aunt Mary!" he whispered. "It's me, Billy!"

The door quickly opened and she peered at him, her confusion turning to delight. "Billy! You're back! I never would've known you. You don't look like yourself at all! Your mom and dad won't believe it! Get in here!"

"Ssh!" Billy touched a finger to his lips. "Don't say anything! I want to surprise them. Don't tell 'em it's me. Take me in and make me a sandwich. See if they know me."

Aunt Mary had always loved practical jokes. Merriment shone on her face. "Come inside. Leave those dirty boots outside the door." As she hustled him along the hallway, she sang out, "Joan, there's a vagrant boy here looking for some lunch."

"Well, take him into the kitchen, Mary. Make him a sandwich," called his mom from upstairs.

He followed her into the kitchen. He was still wearing the socks his mother had knitted for Ed, although now they had holes in heel and toe. He sat down at the table. Mary cut some bread and laid out luncheon meat and a glass of juice, whispering to him and giggling. As he ate, his mother called again down the hallway.

"Everything okay, Mary?"

She came in holding some folded tea towels to put in a drawer. She glanced at him. "And give him a piece of pie before he goes. He looks real skinny."

He stole a quick look at his mother before ducking his head to eat his sandwich. She looked the same, but he saw worry in her eyes as she bustled here and there, brushing a stray curl away in that familiar gesture. There were six chairs around the table so he guessed they had enough paying guests to keep them going.

She hurried out and he grinned to himself as he looked down at his clothes. Even his shirt was unrecognizable with its faded soiled cotton, though it was a shirt she had sewn for Ed.

"We have to tell her," whispered his aunt. "She'll never guess."

But he shook his head, no.

As Billy ate the slice of pie, his mother walked back in and gave him a closer look. He said nothing and kept his head down.

"You must be real hungry," she offered. "Make sure you give him seconds, Mary."

His aunt stifled a giggle. "I'll be sure to do that."

"Thank you, ma'am," Billy said.

She hesitated, puzzled, then peered at him closely, the knowledge just beginning to dawn in her eyes.

"Well, it's coming to something when a mother don't even know her own son!" he said, pretending anger, then burst into laughter as she gave a scream and sat down hard in a chair.

"William Knight! It *is* you! You about gave me a heart attack. Come over here and give your mother a kiss, then tell me where you've been."

Billy got up to hug and kiss her though she shrank a little from the dust on his face. Then he hugged his aunt Mary, and looked around for his father.

"Dad home?"

"He's having a nap. He'll be awake soon."

At their urging he launched into stories about his travels, and about Ed and Kitty, but he didn't dare mention his part in the riot. He would wait to tell his father about that.

"So Ed's got a girl, eh?" said his mother. "He's too young to settle down, especially in these times." She got up from the table. "I was hoping you'd see sense and come back, Billy. I was so frightened for you out there alone. Come upstairs and I'll show you where we put your bed and your things. It's a little room but if we rent it out, we'll move you into the attic space. Come on. You need a bath and some clean clothes."

Billy got up to follow her but paused. He had to break the news and better now than later. She had to realize he had changed from the boy who had set out that early morning, months ago. Since then, he'd been accepted by a band of Trekkers, strong men who had counted him as one of them. "Wait, Mom," he said, and she turned to him with a questioning look.

He forged ahead. "I'm not a little kid, anymore. I can take care of myself. I'm just back for awhile, then I'm moving on."

"Billy! No ..." his aunt sighed.

He could see alarm in his mother's eyes, but it was only fair to tell her. "I'm gonna head east, find some work near the ocean, on the ships, maybe. There's nothing here."

She shook her head and sat down again. "Billy, please stay. There's something you don't know. Your father needs your help. He's not been well."

Billy felt a rush of fear. "Because of me? Where is he? I'll go see him."

"No, nothing to do with you," she assured him. "He had a stroke. All the worry of losing the farm was too much. You can see him when he wakes up after his nap."

"It's really bad? Will he get better?"

"He's getting better. He needs some cheering up and he'll be glad of your help. We both need you here. Your Aunt Mary and Uncle Tom have moved to Watrous to be close to the grandchildren." She threw a grateful look toward her sister. "Mary's here to help out for a little while till Dad recovers, but now you're home, you can step in, Billy, and start school again. Mrs. Lundquist is back teaching in the fall now there's money to pay her."

He felt a sharp worry for his father mixed with the groaning awareness that his mom and dad needed him. Really, really needed him. He felt as if he had decked the wrong freight train, one that was slowing down and chugging into a siding to sit for a long time.

"Okay, Mom," he said at last, though it pained him to agree. "I'll do it. But first, you gotta promise me one thing."

"What's that?"

"You gotta promise to call me Bill from now on. I'm not a kid anymore."

His mother gazed at him with tenderness. "I can see you're grown up now, son. I'll try to remember."

Billy took a bath and put on some clean clothes. On the way downstairs, he caught sight of himself in the hall mirror. His shirt and pants hung loosely—he'd lost some weight and had grown a little, too. His wrists hung out past the ends of his shirtsleeves. He steeled himself for changes in his father's appearance as he hurried into the parlour.

He found his dad sitting near the fireplace where warming flames danced. It was not his broken body that Billy saw first of all, but the look of joyful surprise on his father's face. For a brief second, Billy saw what he himself would become with his father's guidance—a man of substance and courage, someone capable of rooting out each and every golden moment amongst all the hardships. And in that second, he felt again the familiar loving bond with his dad that he had always known and that would never break. He vowed to stand by him. They would meet this setback together, father and son, and this would be the only journey he needed.

CHAPTER 22

CALL TO WAR

"Name!"

"Bill Knight."

"Age?"

"Going on eighteen."

The recruiting officer looked him over. "You got your parents' signatures for permission?"

His parents had refused at first, but he'd browbeaten them until they'd given in.

"Yes, sir! Right here."

"How's your eyesight?"

"Sharp. Real sharp."

"Okay, young fellow. Step inside. The doc will examine you. Sign here."

The officer's stamp came down over his signature. It was official. He was free to go to war. Ed had already beaten him to it. A year ago, his brother had enlisted with the South Saskatchewan Regiment and been among the first of the Canadian troops to sail to Europe. He and Ed might battle together again soon, just as they had in Regina. The idea gave him the same thrill as when he had first decked a freight train and known the force of it hurtling him into the unknown. Five years had passed since then. After their defeat in Regina, the Trekkers had experienced a grand victory over Prime Minister Bennett. They and thousands of others had voted him out of office. Bill imagined how loudly the men must have cheered at the good news.

Bill had stayed put in his hometown just as he had promised, and he had played by the rules—school, girlfriends, hard work. But he had hidden away the secret that deep inside him still lay a wanderlust, like live embers needing only a stir to burst into flame. And he had never forgotten Tiny.

Now he boarded a bus, excited to share his news with his mom and dad. Along the route he noticed new patches of green in the fields. The land was healing again after the long plague of drought and dust. He remembered Venn's first downpour when large drops had bounced against the dry ground. He had seen young children who had never experienced a rainfall, run outside squealing with pleasure, palms upturned and mouths open to catch this gift from the sky.

The bus pulled into town and Bill stepped smartly along the street to give his parents the news. He was to be a soldier, and proud of it. His father greeted him at the door and shook his hand with a formality that was new to him. The paralysis had mostly gone from his dad's right side. Only his limp remained. But the marks of struggle still showed plain on his face—the stroke had left its imprint.

"You could have waited a year to please your mother. But we're proud of you," he said, his arm around Bill's shoulders as he led him into the house.

"Is that Bill?" called his mother from the kitchen.

She had protested strongly when Bill had first told them of his plans to enlist. "You men," she had complained. "I don't know why you think war is all glory and heroics."

Now she hurried into the parlour, anxiety plain on her face. "So it's done. When do you leave?" She held herself stiffly, as if preparing for the next blow.

"Tomorrow, Mom."

"You'll be needing some clean clothes," she said, turning away without another word.

"She'll be all right," said his dad. "Where are you training? Regina?"

"That's right. I can see Kitty on my time off. See how fast my niece is growing."

Bill glanced over at the wedding photo of his brother and sister-in-law. Kitty was just like a real sister to him. It would be good to see her and the baby again.

"Heard from Ed this morning," said his father. "Letter's on the sideboard—says it's about time you caught up with him. He's at a base camp in England. Try and look him up when you get over there. Or maybe the war will be done by then."

But the wheels of war spun faster and faster like a runaway freight. After ten weeks of training, Bill spent some time at home to say goodbye. On his last morning, he awoke before dawn and gathered his things as his parents slept. They'd held a farewell party for him the night before. It felt easiest to slip out now without any fuss, an echo from his hobo days. He scribbled a note and left it on the kitchen table.

I'll be back when I've beat the hell out of Hitler.

He crept through the parlour and found his father snoozing on the couch. A creak in the floorboards woke him and he yawned and stood up to stretch.

"Bill, you all set? Wanted to make sure I saw you off with some cash on hand." He reached into his pocket and proffered some bills. "Here, take this to see you on your way."

"Thanks, Dad." Bill took the folded money and tucked it away, wordless and swept by a rush of emotion.

His dad held out his arms and enclosed him tight in a loving embrace. "Goodbye, son. It's going to be a tough road for you. Keep on the lookout for good surprises along the way."

—

Toronto ... Kingston ... Chenier ... Rivière du Loup ... Rimouski ... Bill jotted down the names of the passing villages and towns on his train journey eastward. Every window in the troop train was covered, but he and the other soldiers secretly peeked out through a gap in the curtains now and again. He caught glimpses of snow-laden fir trees, a hill of crosses, and little boats on a river. He saw cars with chains on their wheels to help navigate icy slopes, and once he saw a boisterous party right on a station platform, complete with an accordion player, singers and dancers.

"I'm catching up to you Ed," he wrote in his journal. *"Wait for me! We'll fight Hitler together!"*

After two days of travel, his train pulled into Pier 21. He and the men mustered on the platform, weary from the journey. He enjoyed the sudden rush of sea air and glimpsed the grey rainy skies over Halifax as he waited for roll call. Then he marched with the others into the great hall and up the stairs to the second floor. There, Bill laid down his kit bag on one of five hundred cots filling the large room.

He and the others were free to explore the city for a few hours before supper. Tonight, a group of Halifax entertainers would present a concert party on an old rusty boat in the harbour. Bill knew the music would lift all their spirits on this last night in Halifax. He felt the same eagerness as the others to begin his journey across the Atlantic.

But he drew deck watch duty that evening and though it cut into his chance to enjoy the musical show, he was happy to patrol and take in the view of the Atlantic Ocean and the Halifax skyline. He could almost believe the clock had turned back and he was a boy again, standing at the edge of the Pacific with a band of men who would become his friends in the battle to make a better world.

But this was a different time and place without the peace of that moment in Vancouver. Sounds of singing and cheering drifted toward him from the mess hall. The happy music on board blended with the clamorous din from the port—the pounding of rivet guns and the flare of welding torches as workers repaired ships damaged by enemy attacks and storms. Military planes roared overhead, while alongside the piers he heard the constant chug of locomotives carrying troops and supplies to waiting ships that filled the harbour. Tomorrow, he and hundreds of others would board one of those and join a convoy that would cross the Atlantic to Great Britain.

He listened to the competing sounds of war and revelry, then relieved of his watch, he turned to join the others in the mess hall. His eyes were drawn to a motion below and he stooped to look over the side. He saw a rush of colour on the wharf, like a whirling mirage moving toward the ship—blue dress, purple vest, red hat with a downward tilt that covered the face. Whatever or whoever it was stopped when it reached his ship, the whole assembly a portrait of outrage, and its voice rang out like pealing bells.

"What's a girl expected to do. Climb a ladder in a skirt and heels? I got talent but I'm not a circus act! Give a girl a hand, will ya?"

Bill felt a peculiar tug at his memory, leaned over the rail to get a closer look.

"You can do it, Miss, long as you keep at least one hand and one foot on the rungs, you'll be fine. Come on up. They're waiting for you."

A stream of mutters and curses followed but she made her way up with relative ease like she'd done it a thousand times before. Bill leaned over to take her hand and help her on deck, noticing her index finger had a slight bump and a crookedness, as if broken and set wrong.

All he could see of her was a mop of yellow hair beneath the hat, a slash of red lipstick, a petite wiry body, and a way of holding herself that suggested a grenade was about to explode.

"Which way?" She scarcely looked at him but stood tapping her toe and waiting for directions.

He hesitated, trying to take her in. She glanced up at him from beneath the hat brim and he saw her eyes, blue as a prairie sky.

"Quick now. I'm late."

"Second door on your left down that way."

He watched her moving away from him. She'd filled out since he'd last seen her, developed a sway to her hips, her blonde curls bouncing. He shook himself awake.

"Tiny!"

Turn around. Turn around. Look at me.

She stopped in mid-stride and tossed her head in a way he remembered, and he saw the familiar fire flash for a moment in those eyes as she turned and stared hard at him.

"Why, I know you ..." She took a step toward him. "Rip? What the hell are you doing dressed up like a soldier? Well, sure looks better on you than them dirty rags you had on last time I saw you."

A head popped out of an open door behind her as the sound of laughter and music swelled. A voice called, "Charlotte, get in here. You're holding up the show. They're waiting."

"I—I thought you were dead," he stammered. So much to tell her and no time. No *time*!

"Charlie! You're on! Leave the boy alone and hurry up!"

"Do I look dead?" She looked down at herself in mock surprise, shook her finger at him. "I got a bone to pick with you, Billy Knight. Didn't think to jump off that freight and come looking for me, did ya?"

"I thought ..."

"Even Miss Janet couldn't believe it when I told her. So just maybe I wasn't dead. Maybe ..."

"Wait a minute, Tiny, let me ex—"

Louder now, emphasis on every syllable. "... maybe I was just knocked out on that track with my head cut open. Ever think of *that*?"

"Charlie, get on stage! Do I have to drag you in here?"

"... but did you come looking for me? Nope. Well, you're not getting away so easy this time, Mr. Billy Knight. You come find me after the show. I'll be in the dressing room—if you got one on this old bucket of a ship."

She turned and marched through the open door and he felt as if a flash fire had swept by him, leaving him singed, and shaken, and exhilarated and ... happy. God, was he happy! He heard cheers and whistles as her familiar voice, rich and full now, broke into song. Her eyes fixed on him as he stepped inside the door for another look at her, shocked by the sudden current of life coursing through him.

He sailed on a troop ship the next morning with nine hundred others, her photograph and an address in his pocket. As he watched his homeland disappear over the horizon, he believed the tides of change must surely turn again, perhaps soon, perhaps in the distant future. But life offered him one constant. He could look beyond war and its machinery, see the peace and love, the cycles of growth and renewal that awaited him on his return.

And he would return. Together they would have lots of time to live and laugh at it all, and hundreds of miles of track yet to travel.

ACKNOWLEDGMENTS

I'm grateful to my insightful editor, Beverley Brenna of Red Deer Press, who cheered me on. Thanks to the following who helped me to navigate the historical events during the 1930s: Chak Yung, Archivist, City of Vancouver; Derek Hayes, author; Donna Sacuta, Executive Director, BC Labour Heritage Centre; Duane Porter, Curator, Halifax & Southwestern Railway Museum, Nova Scotia; Lauren Buttle, Archivist, Royal BC Museum, Victoria; Lorinda Fraser, Archivist, Royal BC Museum, Victoria; Nanci Francis; Paige Hohmann, Archivist, University of BC, Okanagan Campus; Richard Forrest, Chair, Lytton Museum and Archives Commission; William Andrew "Bill" Waiser, PhD, Distinguished Professor Emeritus, affiliate, University of Saskatchewan; Tela Purcell, Glenna Jenkins, Gill Osmond, Diana Dines, Francene Cosman, and Gab Halasz, and to my partner in crime, Robert, for his encouragement and advice.

CREDIT: PETER ZWICKER, LUNENBURG

— · INTERVIEW WITH · —
CHRISTINE WELLDON

What made you want to tell the story of a young character riding the rails during the Great Depression? One of my family members rode the rails across Canada when she was a teenager during the time of flower children and peaceful protests. Her descriptions of the journey were fascinating— the sparks from the clash of steel on steel only visible at night, for example, or the excitement engendered by never knowing what each day would bring. Later, I read that 250,000 children crossed North America during the Great Depression. Many of them were boys like Billy. A few were girls pretending to be boys to survive. The question "What if ...?" has always proven to be a good start to any story a writer is contemplating. What if a teenager sets off on a journey to seek adventure, motivated by the haunting call of a train whistle? What if he discovers important truths along the way that ultimately change him? I saw lots of possibilities in this storyline. The fact that I have a railway museum in my Nova Scotia town helped too!

Tell us about Billy. Why did you choose a teenage boy to tell your story?

During the Dirty Thirties, unemployed men could only drift across the country, seeking jobs that did not exist. Thousands were teenagers only slightly older than Billy. As a hopeful young teen, Billy is representative of those young drifters who began their journey with excited anticipation. Billy naïvely expects to earn a hundred dollars and buy a car, but his hopes are shattered as he comes to realize what the older men already know—he has no hope of finding work. Through Billy's eyes we see the privations that came with failing crops, dust and grasshoppers. And while his story recounts a physical journey, it also explores his journey to maturity.

Your story centres on the connection Billy forges with Tiny. Did girls really ride the rails in the Thirties?

Yes, indeed. Girls like Tiny left their homes whether by necessity or a hankering after adventure. When faced with extreme poverty, mothers resorted to using Quaker Oats Flour sacks to stand in for dresses when there were no pennies for cloth, or buttons, or sewing thread. To escape such poverty, some girls left home to travel with boyfriends, while others dressed as boys to survive. Billy is a much different person at the end of the story than the beginning, owing to, among other factors, his interaction with characters like Tiny. Initially believing girls have no gumption, Billy discovers their strength through the characters of Tiny and Kitty, Evvie, Katie, Mrs. Cooper, and others. And while Billy's story recounts a physical journey, it also explores his journey to emotional maturity.

Your story describes the jungles of older hobos, but you also write about children who travel in gangs. Was that true of this era?

In my research, I found many first-hand accounts of children who sheltered together in camps, and travelled on down the line when threatened. Spike's gang is a true portrayal of how these gangs "glaumed" and "gooseberried" to stay alive under the guidance of a leader who controlled the take. In describing the gang, I referenced Charles Dickens's fictional character, Fagin and his band of pickpockets from the novel *Oliver Twist*. The kid gangs of the Depression were really not much different than Dickens's brilliant portrayal of such children during the 1800s in London. My character Tiny is fashioned after the "Artful Dodger" in that novel, but I gave him a certain "twist" of his own.

What was the significance of the Regina Riot of 1935? Why did you want to build your story around true events?

I wanted to illustrate that social change can happen from the grassroots level. The Trekkers changed public opinion. At first considered by others to be homeless drifters and hobos, they evolved into an organized army of young men who rightfully demanded that the existing government help bring the quality of life they deserved. Though they initially failed in their mission, they drew attention to the unfairness, indignities, and social injustice inflicted on them by the workcamps, and eventually they swayed public opinion, an event that helped to oust Prime Minister Bennett from office. It shows that anyone can help shape the world into a better place by making small changes now. You can be a changemaker, too!

Many of the characters in your story were dissatisfied with Prime Minister Bennett. Why was this?

Those suffering from poverty due to the stock market crash, and especially those in the prairie provinces who suffered from drought, dust, and crop failure, were very angry with their prime minister, because at first he did nothing to help them. Bennett believed it was up to the provinces and communities to help their citizens. Canadians in general viewed him as a millionaire banker who had no understanding or empathy for the ordinary person.

Hobos put the blame squarely on Bennett for their being unemployed and homeless. They shared a grim humour about their prime minister. When they used newspaper padding to keep warm, they called them "Bennett blankets". A "Bennett barnyard" was an abandoned farm, and a "Bennett coffee" was a cup of hot water poured over roasted wheat grains. The most famous of these names was the "Bennett buggy," a car pulled by a horse, since there was no money to pay for gasoline.

Bennett tried to help, but he made the situation worse when he created work camps for single young unemployed men. The federal government paid these workers a very low daily wage, and set them to work at tasks that had no meaning or usefulness, serving only to keep the men busy and off the streets. Many people wrote personal letters to Bennett, begging for help to feed their families. Bennett was a kind man, and he wrote hundreds of letters in return. You can read these letters on a website called "Dear Mr. Prime Minister."

https://www.cbc.ca/history/EPISCONTENTSE1EP13 CH2PA3LE.html

In the town of Biggar, Billy and Tiny are captivated by a travelling entertainment troupe called Chautauqua. Can you tell us about this troupe?

Chautauqua is an Iroquois word meaning "two moccasins tied together,"— a term that might describe Billy and Tiny as they set out on their adventures as a duo. The Chautauqua troupe began in the United States as a travelling tent show, then reached Canada in 1935, when this story takes place.

Chautauqua was an education and social movement that brought entertainment to small communities and cities across the country. It included speakers, lecturers, singers, actors, musicians and show people. The front rows inside the big tent were always given to children so they were close to the stage. If they were watching a play that had a villain in the story, children would hurl peanut shells at the stage actor. Julius Caesar was the name of a real performer—Julius Caesar Nayphe, whose speeches were so popular, people often followed him from town to town across the province.

In Regina, Billy experiences a terrible battle between the police force and the Trekkers. What happened at the end of this battle?

The Regina Riot resulted in the arrests of 140 Trekkers and civilians who helped them. It caused the deaths of one police-man, Charles Miller, and one Trekker, Nick Schaack as well as thousands of dollars worth of damage to the city. Hundreds of Trekkers were injured and, like Ed, ended up in hospitals, or private homes, or jail. While the police accused the Trekkers of firing guns, this later proved to be untrue. No Trekkers fired shots. The Riot was bad news for Bennett's government, and his party lost the 1935 federal election.

Did the Trekkers' mission fail? Had it been all for nothing?
The Regina Riot called attention to the social problems of
Canadians during the Great Depression. The riot won many
sympathizers to the Trekkers' cause. It led to the end of federal
work camps for the unemployed. It highlighted the need for a
minimum wage much higher than the work camp wages offered,
and it eventually helped win reforms in the areas of health care
and unemployment insurance. These reforms came about in the
following years under Prime Minister William Mackenzie King.

Trekkers were proud to have given their all to this cause,
and many continued to push for change. In the words of one
Trekker, "We were pretty militant, but we had a reason to be. If
you were going hungry in the richest country in the world, *you*
would have done it, too."

**You included a real-life character in your story, a
Canadian leader and idealist, Arthur "Slim" Evans who
led two thousand Trekkers in a battle for fair wages
and fair treatment. Can you tell us more about his life?**
At the age of thirteen, Arthur Evans left school to go to work
and support his family. He spent his adult life as a union leader
fighting for justice for the downtrodden. He was arrested and
imprisoned several times in his life, pursued by the Ku Klux
Klan, and on one occasion, a strikebreaker shot him in the leg

with a machine gun, causing a permanent limp. He joined the Communist Party in Canada. Slim's initiatives brought much needed reform to the workcamps of the 1930s, as well as the eventual defeat of Prime Minister Bennett. After the riot in Regina, Evans continued his work toward social justice. His life was abruptly cut short at the age of 53 in 1944, when he was struck and killed by a Vancouver streetcar.

Why did you include the Métis character, Jerry Marcel, as someone Billy meets during one of his many adventures? Were there sensitivities you navigated in creating Jerry that you'd like readers to think about?

The Métis and other Indigenous peoples suffered violence at the hands of the white conquerors and settlers during Canada's beginnings and such racism and bigotry exists today. Railroad bulls and other white drifters punished African Americans and African Canadians along with Indigenous peoples riding the rails much more severely than they punished white people. I focused on a Métis character because my story is centred in western Canada. I consulted with a Métis advisor who supported the accuracy of this passage. When I described this very brief episode about Jerry, I was limited to present only a surface picture within the narrow confines of one chapter. Further information is available in the written and documented history of Indigenous peoples and I encourage my reading audience to explore these. I have included some titles in my suggested reading list.

Billy eventually enlists as a soldier at the start of World War II. Why did you decide to add this detail at the end of his story?

You might look at the "Dirty Thirties," as a decade that was book-ended by the stock market crash on one end, and World War II at the other. The stock market crash caused unemployment and poverty at the start of the decade, while the World War at decade's end provided a boost for Canada's economy. The war industry created thousands of jobs for the 529,000 unemployed people across Canada, offering new opportunities for work in munitions factories, the militia, ship building, defense, and nursing, to name just a few. Canada's entry into the war put people back to work and breathed new life into the economy.

This story begins on the prairie landscape of Saskatchewan, extends west into Alberta and British Columbia and eventually crosses eastward to Atlantic Canada. How did you go about writing these sections? Have you travelled to all these places?

I've lived in a number of provinces in Canada from the Atlantic to Pacific coasts and visited the rest, except for Nunavut and the

Yukon territories. The regional differences in speech and lifestyles among the provinces and territories are remarkable, each with a distinct personality—from laid back to supersonic speed, from gentle to powerful. It is fascinating how history, landscape, and climate shape the character of a country's people. I hope I have accurately presented the physical journey Billy takes. I spoke to many people across Canada about the culture, climate and geography of the places where they live. I'm always breathless when I see the magnificence that every region of Canada offers.

Is there anything else you'd like our readers to know here about your writing process?

As a writer, I'm always attuned to the voices of people who experienced extraordinary events throughout history. I'm compelled to write about how the children of each era navigated such events. Most of my books, both fiction and nonfiction, feature this approach, whether about the sinking of the Titanic, the destruction of Africville, or arriving as a new immigrant through Pier 21. It is a way to learn about distant historical events in a more personal and immediate way, and to appreciate the resilience of the people who helped or are still helping to shape Canada.

—· CITATIONS ·—

Bliss, Phillip Paul, composer. "Hold the Fort" (1898). John Church Co., Cincinnati, 1898. Notated Music. https://www.loc.gov/item/ihas.200001207/.

Chapin, Edward Hubbell, composer. "Bury Me Not on the Lone Prairie" (1839). AFS 05677 B02.

Gillespie, Haven, Seymour Simons, and Richard Whiting, composers. "Breezin' Along With the Breeze" (1926). *Vocal Popular Sheet Music Collection*. Score w2819.

—· SUGGESTED READING LIST ·—
(from picture books to non-fiction)

I Lost My Talk, by Rita Joe; Nimbus Publishing Limited

Northwest Resistance, by Katherena Vermette; HighWater Press

What the Eagle Sees: Indigenous Stories of Rebellion and Renewal, by Eldon Yellowhorn and Kathy Lowinger; Annick Press

Fiddle Dancer, by Wilfred Burton and Anne Patton; Strong Nations Publishing

Gabriel Dumont, by George Woodcock; Strong Nations Publishing

Louis Riel Day: The Fur Trade Project, by Deborah L. Delaronde; Strong Nations Publishing

Children of the Great Depression, by Russell Freedman; Clarion Books

Nowhere to Call Home, by Cynthia C. DeFelice; HarperCollins

Six Days in October: The Stock Market Crash of 1929, by Karen Blumenthal; A Wall Street Journal Book for Children

That Scatterbrain Booky, by Bernice Thurman Hunter; Scholastic Canada

The Mystery of the Hobo's Message, by Elspeth Campbell Murphy; Bethany House Publishers

All Hell Can't Stop Us: The On-to-Ottawa Trek and Regina Riot, by Bill Waiser; Fifth House Publishers

Iron Road West: An Illustrated History of British Columbia's Railroads, by Derek Hayes; Harbour Publishing